The Seduction of Alex Parker

Sandi Lynn

Sandi Lynn

The Seduction of Alex Parker

Cover Design by Cassy Roop @ Pink Ink Designs

Photography by Sara Eirew @ Sara Eirew Photography

Models: Philippe Lemire & Jennie Lyne

Editing by B.Z. Hercules

Urban Dictionary Definitions:

Douchebag: NoMerci366

Bye Felicia: pimpin'817

Love: jo813

Books by Sandi Lynn

If you haven't already done so, please check out my books. They are filled with heartwarming love stories, some with millionaires, and some with just regular everyday people who find love when they least expect it.

Millionaires:

The Forever Series (Forever Black, Forever You, Forever Us, Being Julia, Collin, A Forever Family)

Love, Lust & A Millionaire (Wyatt Brothers, Book 1)

Love, Lust & Liam (Wyatt Brothers, Book 2)

His Proposed Deal

Lie Next To Me (A Millionaire's Love, Book 1)

When I Lie with You (A Millionaire's Love, Book 2)

A Love Called Simon

Then You Happened

Second Chance Love:

Remembering You

She Writes Love

Love In Between (Love Series, Book 1)

The Upside of Love (Love Series, Book 2)

Table of Contents

Books By Sandi Lynn..3

Chapter 1..6

Chapter 2..12

Chapter 3..19

Chapter 4..24

Chapter 5..30

Chapter 6..35

Chapter 7..40

Chapter 8..46

Chapter 9..53

Chapter 10..59

Chapter 11..65

Chapter 12..72

Chapter 13..78

Chapter 14..85

Chapter 15..91

Chapter 16..98

Chapter 17..106

Chapter 18..113

Chapter 19..119

Chapter 20..126

Chapter 21..135

Chapter 22..143

Chapter 23..150

Chapter 24 158
Chapter 25 166
Chapter 26 171
Chapter 27 178
Chapter 28 185
Chapter 29 192
Chapter 30 199
Chapter 31 204
Chapter 32 210
Chapter 33 215
Chapter 34 222
Chapter 35 228
Chapter 36 234
Chapter 37 241
Chapter 38 247
Chapter 39 253
Chapter 40 259
Chapter 41 265
Chapter 42 270
Chapter 43 276
Chapter 44 282
Chapter 45 287
Chapter 46 291
About The Author 299

Chapter 1

Emerson

Never stay in one place too long. That was my motto. There was so much of the world to see on what little time we had left, and that was exactly what I planned to do. Until my money started to run out. Sitting in my box of an apartment in Texas, I picked up my phone and called my brother, Adam.

"Hello, Emerson."

"Hey, big brother. Listen, I need some more cash."

"Em, you're done. Your money is pretty much depleted. You told me you were going to settle in one place and get a job."

"I had a job. I quit. It's time to move on. I'm over Texas, Adam, and I need to leave."

I heard him sigh. "Emerson, you're twenty-six years old. It's time to stop what you're doing and settle down somewhere. Make a place your permanent home. I thought we talked about this already."

"Adam, I need some money to leave Texas. I can't stay here anymore."

"What happened to that cowboy you were seeing? I thought things were serious between the two of you."

"Nah. He was nice and all, but he was getting too serious. He started talking about marriage and kids. Do you see now why I need to leave?"

"You can't keep going on like this, Em. The answer is no. You're not getting any more money because there isn't any. I warned you about this a year ago. Damn it. It's time you grew up."

"I am grown up. Just because I don't like to be stuck in the same place and live a boring, ordinary life like most people do, doesn't mean I'm a child."

"It's always the same argument with you."

"Fine, Adam. Leave me homeless." *Click.*

I threw my phone down on the couch and paced around the room. I was going crazy here in Texas and I needed to leave ASAP. I had other places to go. He didn't understand. He couldn't understand. No matter how many times I tried to explain it, he didn't want to hear it. Just because he was happy being cooped up in an office working a nine to five job didn't mean shit.

The next morning, as I was drinking my coffee and dodging calls from Billy, my phone rang. It was Adam.

"What?" I answered in a huff.

"Watch that tone of yours, little sister. Listen, I've been thinking that you need to come back to California for a while. We need to sit down and have a talk."

"You mean you need to sit down and lecture me? And I don't want to go back there."

He sighed. "My job is relocating me to Tennessee for the next three months to try and save a company that's going under. I've bought a plane ticket for you and you're going to stay with a friend of mine. His name is Alex Parker."

"Why can't I stay at your place? If I decided to come back."

"Because it's being renovated while I'm gone and it will be unlivable."

"So you want me to stay with a guy friend of yours? What brother does that to his sister? Tells her to move in with a total stranger?"

"Trust me. You have nothing to worry about with Alex. Besides, he owes me a favor and I called it in last night. Three months, Em, and then I'll be back and we're going to talk. But, within those three months, you are to figure out your damn life and decide where you're going to plant yourself in this world and stay. Alex's house is huge and he's never home, so you'll barely see him."

"I don't know about this, Adam. I don't want to come back and you know that."

"Do you want to get out of Texas or not? This is your only option," he spoke with seriousness.

"Fine." I sighed. "I'll come to California. When is my flight?"

"Tomorrow morning at eight a.m. So get packing."

"Will I see you tomorrow?"

"No. I'll be gone before your flight gets in. I'll text you Alex's address. Just take a cab there and get yourself settled. I'll be back in three months."

I rolled my eyes. "Okay. Since you have my life all figured out for me, I guess I have no choice."

"Have a safe flight and I'll talk to you soon." *Click.*

I loved my brother. He was all I had left in this world, but sometimes, he could be a real asshole and he was being an asshole now by making me come back to California.

****

Alex

I met Adam for dinner and a drink before he left for Tennessee. I couldn't believe I agreed to let his little sister stay at my place while he was gone.

"Thanks again for letting Emerson stay with you, man."

"No problem. What are friends for? Right?" I gave an unsure smile.

"I think I should warn you about her. She's kind of a free spirit. She can be very mouthy and defiant. But she has a heart of gold and she can cook. I already told her you're never home, so the two of you probably won't see each other anyway."

"True. Don't worry. I'll make sure she feels at home. Actually, I'll have Jenna make sure she feels at home. It's only for three months, right?"

"Yes. As soon as I get back, I will come collect my sister, and I apologize in advance for anything crude or rude she may say to you."

I chuckled. "I'll let you know when you get back if I accept your apology."

****

"Jenna, we will be having a house guest for the next three months. Her name is Emerson and she's my friend Adam's little sister. Please make sure one of the guest rooms is fixed up for her, and when she arrives, show her around. Her flight gets in this afternoon. I'll be at the office and I'm not sure when I'll be home. Also, please make sure she doesn't touch anything valuable."

"Of course, Mr. Parker." She nodded.

I climbed into the back seat of the Bentley and told my driver, Phillip, about Emerson.

"If you're not driving me around and Miss James needs to go somewhere, please see to it she gets to her destination safely. If she asks you to take her somewhere absurdly far, consult me first."

"Not a problem, Alex. I must say that I'm really surprised you're letting her stay with you. That isn't like you to have house guests."

I sighed. "I'm doing a favor for a friend. Trust me. I won't be doing this again."

He smiled and drove me to my office. I was feeling unsure about this situation and I forgot to ask Adam how old his sister was and he never mentioned it. But he warned me about her being mouthy and defiant, so I guessed she was around eighteen. Just what I needed: a kid hanging around the house. I'd have to set some rules and she would follow them or else. The weird thing about Adam was that he never spoke of his family. I'd known him for three years and this was the first I heard about a sister. He was a good guy and did me a huge favor a year ago. When he called me and asked me if Emerson could stay with me, I couldn't exactly turn him down.

Chapter 2

Emerson

As soon as I stepped off the plane and my feet hit the ground in California, my breathing became restricted. I needed to find a bathroom and get myself under control. The memories here were bad and I had left for a reason. Damn Adam for bringing me back. I had thc tinicst bit of hope that being away for eight years would have made things easier. But I was wrong. Dead wrong.

Walking to baggage claim, I grabbed my two large suitcases and got into a cab. Showing the driver my phone, I asked him to take me to the address Adam sent me. I was surprised that the address was in Malibu. Who was this Alex Parker? Time to google him and find out. My eyes literally popped out of my head when I searched him. He was *the* Alex Parker. A well-known, world-famous real estate developer. He owned just about everything. Hotels, mortgage companies, apartment buildings, condos, restaurants, and a couple resorts around the world. Fuck! He was a billionaire and he was only thirty years old. Was that even possible? Damn, he was sexy. Holy shit. How the hell did Adam expect me to stay in the same house with that fine-looking man? But he did say I would have nothing to worry about with Alex, so I bet he was an asshole. An uptight, rich playboy who thought he owned the world type of asshole. As long as he stayed out of my way, I'd stay out of his, and judging by the number of different women he was photographed with, I bet he was a commitment phobe. If he was, at least we had that in common.

Pulling up the long winding driveway, we were stopped by a black wrought-iron gate. The driver pushed the button and the gates opened, allowing him to pull up to the house. He got out and fetched my suitcases from the trunk. I paid him his fare and, when he left, I stood there and stared at the mammoth home, which was situated on a hill. The front door opened and a woman stepped outside. She looked to be in her early thirties, petite, and she wore her black hair in a bun.

"Hello, you must be Miss James. I'm Jenna, Mr. Parker's housekeeper." She gave a warm smile.

I held out my hand. "I'm Emerson. It's nice to meet you."

She took one of my bags and led me inside. Stopping dead in my tracks in the foyer, I looked around at the beautifully decorated home of Mr. Parker. Jenna led me to a bedroom on the first floor towards the back of the house.

"Umm, Jenna. How big is this house?" I asked.

"It's seven thousand square feet."

"Jesus. Who needs a house that big?"

She laughed. "This is your room. You'll have more privacy here and it's the biggest guest room in the house. Plus, it has the best view."

As she opened the door, I gasped. The room was bigger than my apartment back in Texas. Hell, it was bigger than anything I'd ever stayed in. The vaulted ceilings, taupe walls, and white crown molding gave the room a look of pure elegance. A king-sized sleigh bed sat on one wall with a fireplace and a built-in

TV sat above it on the opposite wall. There were French doors that opened and led to a patio that was furnished with a couple of chairs and a table. The curtains were made of silk and hung elegantly to the floor. But it was the view that caught my attention and caught it fast. It overlooked the Pacific Ocean.

"Over here is your closet," Jenna spoke as she opened the double doors.

I lost my breath as I stepped inside the double walk-in closet that housed a beautiful, large, white vanity. Shit, even the closet was bigger than my apartment. It was truly its own living space.

"This is amazing."

Jenna smiled. "Wait until you see the bathroom."

Stepping out of the closet, we walked down a small hallway that led to the bathroom. I'm not kidding when I say I think I had an orgasm. It contained a large, sunken jet tub that was big enough for at least four people, a large glass-encased walk-in shower, and a huge counter with double sinks. The entire bathroom was done in a beige marble and decorated to perfection.

"He didn't decorate this house, did he?" I asked.

"No. Mr. Parker hired an interior decorator to decorate as he built the home."

"How long has he lived here?" I asked out of curiosity.

"About five years. Come with me and I'll show you the rest of the home."

As we walked through the house, Jenna led me to the kitchen and orgasm number two happened. This kitchen was a chef's dream. Holy shit. With the double ovens, the double stove, the large granite island that sat in the center, and the biggest stainless steel refrigerator I'd ever seen, I could see many elegant meals being prepared here. The dark cherry wood cabinets and moldings graced the entire kitchen, framing a large bay window with a cushioned window seat that overlooked the ocean.

After the tour, we stepped outside into the back yard. I had to tighten my legs from orgasm number three. The view, the tree-lined area, infinity pool, hot tub, and many furnishings—all were unbelievable.

"If you go down those steps right there," Jenna pointed to the side, "they will lead you down to the beach."

"This is beautiful. Truly beautiful."

"I know. It's an honor to work here." She smiled.

I looked up to the second story and noticed the wraparound balcony. "What's up there?"

"That floor is where Mr. Parker's bedroom and home office is."

I arched a brow at her. "His bedroom and office is the entire floor?"

"Yes. That floor is off limits. Nobody is allowed up there unless you have permission from Mr. Parker."

"And you?"

"I have to clean up there, so I'm pretty much the only one allowed."

"I see. I have a question. Is Mr. Parker uptight?"

She let out a light laugh. “Yes. Just a bit.”

“Great. Well, at least he’s never home. So I won’t see him much, right?”

“Correct. He does pop in during the day every once in a while. As for night, I really don’t know. I leave every day at five. He is a very social man who spends a lot of his time at charities and events, so he’s really not home much.”

“What a waste to have a house like this and never be able to enjoy it.”

She softly nodded her head. “If you’ll excuse me, I have to get back to work. Mr. Parker said to make yourself comfortable. There’s plenty of food and beverages in the refrigerator if you’re hungry.”

“Thank you, Jenna.”

“You’re welcome, Miss James.”

“No formality. I hate formalities. Call me Emerson.”

“All right, Emerson. If you need anything, please don’t hesitate to ask.”

****

Alex

I arrived home at seven o’clock to meet my houseguest, take a shower and to change for a dinner date I had. When I walked through the door, the most incredible aroma filled the air. I set my briefcase down and walked into the kitchen, where I found a woman wearing extremely short jeans shorts standing over my stove.

"Ahem." I cleared my throat.

She didn't turn around, so I did it again. "Ahem."

I sighed as I walked over to her and tapped her on the shoulder. She jumped and turned around.

"Jesus Christ, you scared me," she said as she took her earphones out.

What the fuck? She was no eighteen-year-old. I stared at her ocean blue eyes as she placed her hand over her heart.

"I tried to speak to you, but obviously, you couldn't hear me." I pointed to her earphones.

"You must be Alex Parker. I'm Emerson James. Adam's sister." She extended her hand.

"Nice to meet you. How old are you?"

"Excuse me?" she asked with a narrowing eye.

"It's just the way Adam talked about you. I thought you were around eighteen. Obviously, by looking at you, you're not."

"I'm twenty-six."

"I see. Okay. Welcome to my home, Miss James, and please make yourself comfortable. I'm assuming Jenna showed you around the property."

"Yes, she did. She was very nice. And what exactly did Adam say about me?" she asked with a furrowed brow.

"Not much. I just assumed you were younger. What are you cooking?" I leaned over and looked in the pot that was sitting on the stove.

"Pasta with a homemade palomino sauce."

"It smells delicious. Adam told me you are quite the cook."

"Would you like some?" she asked with a smile.

Placing my hand in my pocket, I politely told her no.

"I have a dinner date that I need to get ready for. So if you'll excuse me."

"Oh, sure. Have fun."

I turned away and began walking out of the kitchen. Stopping, I turned around and looked at her one last time before heading upstairs. "Thank you."

Fuck oh fuck. Adam's sister was beautiful, extremely beautiful. Her brown hair with blonde highlights that she wore in a ponytail complemented her tanned skin and ocean blue eyes. From what I could see, her body was perfect. She was fit, lean, and toned in all the right places, and the tank top she was wearing clung tightly to her large, round breasts. I shook my head and successfully stopped my cock from getting hard. I was a man, after all, in the presence of a beautiful young woman, and it couldn't be helped. As I stood in the shower, I kept thinking about my cock's reaction to her. Normally, I don't get hard just by looking at a woman like that. I see beautiful women every day and this had never happened before. *What the hell was going on?*

Chapter 3

Emerson

Alex's pictures didn't do him justice. That man was just as delicious-looking in person as he was online. He stood a little over six feet tall with short, sandy-brown hair and brown eyes. His chiseled cheekbones and strong jaw made him very handsome, not to mention the five o'clock shadow that he sported gave way to perfection. *Shit.* And yes, I did look down to his man area to see if he was perhaps sporting anything big. It was too hard to tell in his black suit pants. I'd have to see him in a pair of jeans or maybe a pair of khaki shorts.

As I put my pasta on a plate, and before I stepped onto the patio, I heard the front door open and then shut. *That smell.* I caught a whiff of man scent that drifted into the kitchen. I knew that smell. He had put on Dolce & Gabbana, my favorite man scent of all time. I sighed, grabbed my plate, and took it outside on the patio. It was a beautiful night. The sun had set and the stars were coming out. The warm breeze that swept across my face made me remember how much I used to love living in California. As I was eating, my phone rang. It was Adam.

"Hello."

"Just making sure you arrived safely. How are things going?"

"Fine so far. You didn't tell me that Alex Parker was *the* Alex Parker."

"To be honest, I didn't think about it. Does it matter?"

"No. But his house is like a mansion."

"Yeah. It's pretty cool, isn't it? Hey, are you okay being there? I mean, back in California?"

Oh, now he asks.

"No. Not really, and to be honest, I'm really pissed at you for making me come back here."

"You need to put the past behind you, Em. I know it's hard, but you have to move on with your life."

"I have moved on, Adam! I just chose not to move on here. This conversation goes the same way every time. I have to go." *Click.*

I was getting tired, so I cleaned up and headed to my bedroom. After changing into my pajamas, I opened the French doors to let the breeze blow into the room. Climbing into bed, I pulled the sheet over me and stared out into the night, listening to the waves as they crashed against the shore.

****

I had always been an early riser. As far as I was concerned, there wasn't one minute of the day to be wasted. Climbing out of bed, I slipped into my crème-colored, short silk robe and stepped outside on the patio off my room, breathing in the fresh morning air and looking out into the ocean. A smile crossed my face when I saw two dolphins in the water.

I went into the kitchen and started a pot of coffee. I jumped when my phone started to ring. Who the hell would be calling me this early? Oh. It was Billy. *Shit*. I answered it and put it on speaker as I took the eggs from the refrigerator.

"Hello."

"Where the hell are you, Em? I went to your place last night and you were gone. I tried calling your phone, but it went straight to voicemail."

"I'm in California and I turned my phone off last night."

"California! What the hell are you doing there and why didn't you tell me you were going?"

"I had to come here for my brother and I forgot to mention it."

"Baby, please don't lie to me. I'm sorry for the other night. I didn't mean to upset you."

"You didn't upset me and I'm not lying."

I cracked the eggs in the pan, put a piece of bread in the toaster, and began to slice up some avocados.

"Baby, when are you coming home? We need to sit down and have a serious talk."

Alex walked into the kitchen and looked at my phone and then at me.

"I'm not coming back to Texas, Billy."

"What the fuck do you mean you're not coming back to Texas?!" he yelled.

"Do you not understand English?"

I saw Alex smirk.

"It's over between us, Billy. I'm over Texas. I told you to begin with that I probably wasn't staying very long."

"But, Em, what about us? We had plans, damn it!"

"You had plans, Billy. Plans that you were making without talking to me first. You were just assuming a whole lot of things."

"So you're just going to walk away from our relationship? Do you have any idea how bad I'm hurting right now, baby?"

"For god sakes, stop calling me 'baby' and I'm sorry if I hurt you. I'm moving on, Billy, and I suggest you do the same."

"But, Em, I love you. Please don't do this to us. What can I do to make things right?"

"Billy, it's too early for this and I haven't even had my coffee yet. There's nothing you can do. I'm not coming back and it's over. You deserve better than me. I have to go. I'm sorry." *Click.*

"Coffee?" I asked Alex, who was leaning up against the counter.

"Yes. Coffee would be nice. You're quite the little heartbreaker. I was feeling sorry for Billy." He smirked.

I rolled my eyes as I handed him his coffee cup. "Billy will be just fine. Eggs?" I asked.

"No. I don't have time. I have a meeting. Have a nice day, Miss James."

"Enough with the formalities, Alex. Call me Emerson, Em, Emmie—whatever you want. Just not 'Miss James.'"

He cocked his head and smiled. "I think I'll call you 'heartbreaker.'"

"Ugh." I put my head down on the counter and I heard him chuckle as he walked out.

****

Alex

I guess I didn't need to make any rules since Emerson was a grown adult. A beautiful, grown adult, which ultimately could lead to trouble for me if I wasn't careful. Damn Adam for not telling me how hot she was. Hot or not, she was my friend's sister and I couldn't cross that line. Plus, she wasn't my type. She wasn't… how could I put this nicely? She wasn't upscale enough. The women I dated and fucked were of high society. They were classy, something Emerson seemed to lack. I had standards and, unfortunately, she didn't meet them. Which was a good thing. I couldn't help but wonder, though, why she left Texas the way she did. Listening to her conversation with Billy was quite entertaining and the way she just blew him off was ballsy. The women I'd known weren't like that. They were the Billys of the relationship. Begging and pleading me to stay and always trying to change themselves for me. There was a story behind Emerson James and I couldn't help but wonder just what her story was. Was I going to find out? No. It was none of my business. She was here for three months and three months only. As long as she stayed out of my way and life, I would stay out of hers.

Chapter 4

Emerson

Jenna walked into the kitchen as I was cleaning up.

"Good morning, Emerson. How was your first night here?"

"Good morning. It was great. I slept like a baby in that bed."

She laughed. "Good. Any problems with Mr. Parker?"

I twisted my face at her. "No. Why?"

"Just wondering. He can sometimes be a little, how do I say this, rude and insensitive."

"Oh. So far, he seems okay."

"Good. Have a nice day, Emerson." She smiled as she left the kitchen.

Now that I was back in California, it was time to reconnect with some old friends. Friends I hadn't seen in over eight years, but I kept in contact with here and there over Facebook. Best friends I deserted when I left and never looked back. I went to my room and opened up my laptop, pulling up the page of Christine Howl, my best friend back in high school. She was married now with a kid and living her life as a stay-at-home mom.

"Hi, Christine. I'm back in California for a while and I was hoping we could meet for lunch and catch up."

It was a matter of minutes before she replied back.

"OH MY GOD! I can't believe you're back. Yes! Can you meet for lunch today? I'll call Bayli and see if she's available. I know she'd love to see you."

"Today will be great. How about we meet at one o'clock at the Polo Lounge? We used to love that place."

"Sounds great. I can't wait to see you."

"I can't wait to see you too."

Now I was going to have to call a cab. Walking into the kitchen, I saw a man talking to Jenna.

"Emerson, this is Phillip, Mr. Parker's personal driver."

"It's nice to meet you, Emerson. I actually came here to introduce myself to you. Mr. Parker told me that I'm to drive you wherever you may need to go."

"Really?"

"Yes, really. Just as long as he doesn't need me."

"You have perfect timing, Phillip, because I need to be at the Polo Lounge at one o'clock to meet a friend for lunch."

"All right, the Polo Lounge it is." He smiled. "We should leave around noon, so I'll be back to pick you up."

"Thank you. I appreciate it."

He gave a nod and left. He was a handsome-looking gentleman with his dark brown hair, green eyes, and a light beard. I pegged him to be in his late forties, maybe at the most, fifty. I couldn't believe that Alex had asked him to drive me around. Maybe Alex Parker wasn't such a bad guy after all.

I hopped in the shower, got dressed, and waited for Phillip to pick me up. When he arrived, he opened the door to the Bentley and I slid inside.

"So how long have you been driving for Alex?" I asked.

"About three years." He smiled. "What brings you to California?"

"My brother, Adam. I really didn't have a choice but to come back for a while."

"Come back? Have you lived here previously?"

"Yeah. I grew up in LA."

"Why did you leave?" he asked as he looked at me through his rearview mirror.

"It's a long and boring story."

We finally made it to the Polo Lounge and, as I climbed out of the car, Phillip handed me his phone number.

"Put my number in your phone and either call me or text me when you need to go somewhere. The latest I can pick you up is four o'clock."

"That's fine. If I'm going to be later, I'll just catch a cab back."

"Have a nice lunch with your friends, Emerson."

"Thanks, Phillip."

Before I reached the doors to the restaurant, I heard my name being called from the patio area. When I looked over, I saw Christine and Bayli waving me over to their table.

"Look at you," Christine said as she hugged me. "You look amazing."

"Thanks. So do you."

"Long time no see, friend." Bayli smiled as we hugged. It was like we were the Three Musketeers all over again.

As we were catching up, I glanced over and saw Alex being seated at a table across from us. He was with a beautiful, tall woman. He looked over, and when he saw me, an expression of shock overtook his face. I gave a small smile and continued my conversation with Christine and Bayli. After my second glass of wine, I excused myself to the restroom. When I came out, Alex was standing there waiting for me.

"Umm. Hi. Why are you waiting here in the hallway?"

"What are you doing here?" he asked.

I raised my eyebrow. "Having lunch with my friends."

"What are you doing here?"

"The same thing you are."

This was weird and it was making me uncomfortable.

"I didn't know you had friends in LA."

"Well, now you do. So if you'll excuse me, I'm going to get back to them."

He glared at me for a moment. “Enjoy the rest of your lunch.”

“You too.” I patted his rock-hard chest.

Not too long after I got back to the table, Alex returned to his and continued his conversation with the tall, beautiful woman. I wondered if that was his girlfriend. As the two of them got up from their table to leave, Alex glanced over at me one last time. I pretended not to notice.

****

Alex

When I arrived home later that night around eleven o’clock, I saw Emerson in the pool. I stepped out on the patio and waited for her to finish her laps.

“Going for a late-night swim?” I asked.

“Yeah. It’s a beautiful night out.”

As she climbed out of the pool, I couldn’t help but notice her amazing body in her black bikini. *Fuck.* I grabbed the towel from the chair and handed it to her.

“Are you going to bed anytime soon?” I asked.

“Why? Do you want to join me?”

“Excuse me?” I spoke in shock.

“Relax, Alex. I was kidding.” She laughed. “You should have seen your face.”

“Very funny, Emerson. Sleep well.”

“I intend to. You do the same.”

"I will."

"Good." She smiled.

Chapter 5

Emerson

I was thrashing around in my bed. Calling out for help. I couldn't breathe and my skin was heated. Before I knew it, someone was calling my name and shaking me.

"Emerson, wake up. You're having a bad dream."

I opened my eyes and froze when I saw Alex standing over me. I couldn't catch my breath.

"I'm fine." I sat up.

"You don't look fine. You were having a nightmare. I could hear you screaming all the way upstairs."

"I'm sorry. I didn't mean to wake you."

He sat down on the edge of the bed and the only thing I could focus on was his six-pack, or was it an eight-pack? I couldn't tell because my eyes were still trying to focus on reality.

"Don't worry about that. What was your nightmare about?"

"I don't remember," I lied. "I'm okay now. Please just go back to bed. This is awkward for you to be in here in nothing but your pajama pants and me in my nightshirt."

"Are you sure you're okay?"

"I promise you I'm fine."

He got up from the bed and I gulped as I watched his lean, muscular body walk towards the door. "Sleep well."

"I will. Thank you."

He walked out and shut the door. I reached over and turned off the light, climbing back under the covers. This was the first time I had that nightmare in almost eight years.

The next morning, I got up before the sun rose and went for a run along the beach. The cool morning air awoke my senses and I was feeling good, despite last night's nightmare. As I ran along the beach, I watched the sun rise and thanked God for another beautiful day. When I got back to the house, Alex was in the kitchen, sitting at the island and drinking his coffee. He looked at me in shock as I walked through the door wall.

"I thought you were still asleep."

"Nah. I decided to go for a run and watch the sun rise."

"Oh, well, there's coffee over there if you want some."

I reached in the cupboard and took out a cup. Suddenly, a man walked in the kitchen and went into the refrigerator. I arched my brow as I looked at him and then at Alex.

"Robert, I would like you to meet Emerson James. She's my houseguest for the next three months. Emerson, meet Robert, my chef."

He extended his hand. "It's nice to meet you, Emerson."

"Thank you. It's nice to meet you too."

"I'll be making omelets today. Would you like one?" he asked.

"No thanks. I can make my own." I winked.

Looking over at Alex, he narrowed his eyes at me.

"Robert doesn't like anyone in his kitchen."

"Really? I thought this was your kitchen. And if I recall, I made dinner for me the other night and breakfast yesterday morning. In this kitchen. Your kitchen." I pointed my finger at him.

He studied me, giving me a look that my brother always gave me when he was debating whether or not to say something.

"You will wait until Robert is done making breakfast before starting yours. You are not to be in his way. Do you understand, heartbreaker?"

How dare him. I strutted over to him and whispered in his ear, "Yes, I understand. Call me 'heartbreaker' again and it's your heart I won't be breaking. It'll be your balls. Do *you* understand?" I walked away and went to my room.

****

Alex

Who the hell did she think she was talking to me like that? I got up from the island and followed her into her bedroom.

"Excuse me, Emerson. How dare you speak to me that way. Do you know who you're talking to?"

"Yes. I'm talking to you, Alex Parker. A regular guy with the same shit going on in his head like any other ordinary guy.

Just because you have mega millions, it doesn't give you the right to order people around like that."

Now she really had me mad. "And you have no right speaking to me that way."

"And you have no right calling me 'heartbreaker.'"

I sighed. "I apologize for calling you that."

"And I apologize for saying that I'd break your balls."

"Fine. Apology accepted. But don't ever speak to me that way again."

"You can guarantee I will if you call me something other than 'Emerson' again."

The longer I stayed in her room and argued with her, the angrier I became. I started to walk out and stopped when I reached the door. I turned around and put my finger up.

"You—" I was so angry that I couldn't finish my sentence. She stood there with her arms folded and stared at me. I walked out and went to the dining room to have breakfast.

As I was eating, Robert stepped into the room and asked to speak with me.

"My mother has taken ill and I need to go to see her in Florida. I really don't know how long I'll be gone," he spoke.

"I'm sorry to hear that. When are you leaving?"

"As soon as possible."

"I understand, Robert. Have a safe trip and I hope your mother feels better soon."

"Thank you, sir." He gave a small nod and went back into the kitchen.

Could this day get any worse? As I tried to eat my breakfast, I couldn't get over the fact that Emerson had spoken to me the way she did. No woman had ever spoken to me that way and it would never happen again.

Chapter 6

Emerson

I take back what I said about Alex Parker not being such a bad guy. He was a complete asshole the way he spoke to me in his commanding voice, like I was some sort of child. Maybe I shouldn't have told him what I did, but my defenses had gone up. The only people who had a right to talk to me like that were my parents. I couldn't stop thinking about how he came into my room last night to check on me. As weird as it was having him hover over me in bed, it was a nice gesture on his part. I got the feeling there were two sides of Alex Parker. I just hadn't figured out yet which side was more dominant. I was only here for three months and it wouldn't be difficult to have as little contact with him as possible.

After putting on my bathing suit, and as I was walking out the patio door, I heard Alex call my name.

"Emerson. I need to speak with you for a moment."

I rolled my eyes and turned around to face him.

"Yes, Alex."

"Robert's mother has taken ill and he is leaving for Florida. So I will need you to step in and take his place."

I raised my eyebrow at him. "Take his place? What exactly do you mean?"

"You'll be his replacement chef. Mainly cooking my breakfast in the morning and an occasional dinner."

I laughed uncontrollably. "You're kidding, right? You expect me to cook for you?"

"No and yes. Since you apparently have these mad cooking skills, it will save me from having to hire another personal chef. After all, I am letting you stay here," he spoke with seriousness.

Cocking my head, I stared at him, becoming distracted by his overall sexiness in his tailored business suit and his scent that lingered in the air. *Damn him.*

"Fine. Since you were kind enough to open up your home to me while my brother is away, the least I could do is repay you by cooking your meals." I pretty much had to choke out the words.

"Very good. You'll start tomorrow morning. Breakfast is at 7:30 sharp."

"And if I don't have it ready until 7:31 or perhaps 7:32?"

He took in a sharp inhale. "7:30, Miss James." He walked away without even cracking a smile. I didn't see him the rest of the day or night, which was fine with me. I wasn't particularly liking his attitude.

****

I made sure to wake up nice and early to serve His Majesty his breakfast on time. Just as Alex walked into the kitchen, I plated his quiche with a side of fresh fruit and a homemade banana-nut muffin.

"Good morning," he mumbled.

"Morning. Your breakfast is ready."

"It smells delicious in here. Did you make homemade muffins?"

"Yes. Banana-nut. I hope you like them."

"They aren't my first choice, but I don't mind them."

I rolled my eyes as I set his plate on the table.

"Are you joining me?" he asked as he sat down.

I cocked my head. "Does Robert ever join you?"

"No."

"Then why would I?"

I walked out of the dining room and into the kitchen with a small smile on my face. I poured myself another cup of coffee and took a muffin from the cooling rack. Banana-nut might not have been his first choice, but they sure were mine. As I was cleaning up, Alex brought his plate to the kitchen.

"That was an excellent breakfast."

"It must be those mad cooking skills I supposedly have," I replied as I stood over the sink, washing a pan.

Suddenly, I felt a wave of hot breath over my neck as he came up from behind and leaned close to my ear.

"You have very mad cooking skills and I can't wait to see what you cook up next."

I gulped. His scent was infiltrating my space and it was driving me crazy, not to mention the fabric of his suit that lightly brushed up against my skin.

"Guess you'll have to wait and find out," I spoke without turning around.

My phone, which was sitting on the counter, beeped with a voicemail message. Strange that I hadn't heard it ring. Alex backed up and I reached over and pressed play and hit the speaker button because my hands were wet. It was from a number I didn't recognize.

"Hey, Em, it's Ryan. I got a new number and want you to have it if you change your mind about us and come back to Connecticut. I sure do miss you, baby. I miss the great sex we had and I miss holding you in my arms."

I immediately stopped the message and sighed. *Shit.* I couldn't believe Alex heard that.

"Ryan? Great sex? Another heart you broke?" He snickered.

I took in a deep breath. "The sex wasn't all that great and, yes, another heart I broke. Now if you'll excuse me, I have to finish cleaning up before I head down to the beach."

"Enjoy your day and thank you for breakfast."

"No problem. After all, you are letting me stay in your castle." I gave a small smile.

He walked out of the kitchen and I placed my hands against the counter, pushing myself back. Why the hell would Ryan be calling me after all this time?

****

Alex

Sitting in the car on the way to the office, the only thing on my mind was Emerson, the breakfast she made me, and the two hearts she broke. Why the fuck was I thinking about her so much? She was certainly a beautiful woman. Probably, no, definitely one of the most beautiful women I'd ever laid eyes on, but she was mouthy and disrespectful. Even though I despised those two things about women, she had me curious about her. Something was going on with her and I was going to find out what her story was, whether she wanted to tell me or not. I would give her the opportunity to tell me herself and if she didn't, then I would hire someone to find out for me. She was a woman about whom I shouldn't give a damn. She was my friend's sister. But there was something about her that made me want to know more and my mind wouldn't rest until I found out everything about her.

Chapter 7

Emerson

I couldn't shake the feeling I'd had all day after feeling Alex's hot breath sweep across my neck. The only way to describe it was riveting. Feeling him so close to me, I froze up, almost as if he had cast a spell on me. I was unable to move and take in a breath. When I googled him, the only information that came up was business related. There was nothing that told me about his personal life, except for all the pictures of him with different women. But even those seemed businesslike. They were photos of him attending charities, events, premieres, and the opening of whatever new business he took on. The type of woman he was photographed with was classy, rich, and uptight, just like him. How could I tell? It was easy to spot a bitch. But of course he would be into that type of woman. I wouldn't expect anything less from him. It made me wonder if those women put up with his condescending bullshit and attitude. Too much thinking about Alex Parker was dangerous and a waste of time. I had other things to think about, like when Adam got back and we had our talk, where I was going to venture off to next.

As I was relaxing on the beach, soaking up the sun, and plotting my next move, I heard Jenna calling my name.

"Emerson, Mr. Parker just called and said that he needs you to cook dinner tonight for him and a guest. He'll be home around seven o'clock."

I sighed. "Would this guest be of the female species?"

She laughed. "I would say probably."

"Okay, then. It looks like my time down here on the beach is done for the day. I'll have to call Phillip and have him take me to the grocery store."

I grabbed my towel and my water and headed back up to the house. As I walked to my room to change, I dialed Phillip.

"Hello."

"Phillip, it's Emerson James. I'm going to need a ride to the grocery store. Mr. Parker is having me cook dinner tonight for him and a guest."

"Very well, Emerson. When would you like to go?"

"How fast can you be here?"

"About thirty minutes."

"Okay. I'll be waiting for you."

After changing into my clothes, I went to the kitchen and pulled out a piece of paper and a pen from the drawer. As I sat on the stool next to the island, I began to jot down some items I would need. Just as I was completing my list, Phillip walked in.

"Are you ready to go, Emerson?"

"Yes. I just finished my list."

I climbed into the back of the Bentley and Phillip drove me to the store.

"Are you coming?" I asked him as he held the door open for me and I climbed out.

"Where?" he asked with confusion.

"Into the store. I'll give you half the list and we can split up. The sooner we get what I need, the sooner we can get out of here."

"But, Emerson—"

"No buts, Phil. Let's go."

I heard him sigh as he walked behind me and into the store. I ripped the list in half and handed it to him.

"If you have any questions about these items, just ask." I smiled.

****

I set the table with Alex's fine china and placed two beautiful crystal candlestick holders in the center with red candles to create a romantic ambiance. After all, if he was bringing home his date for dinner, I wanted to make it as romantic as possible for them. Not really. I just did it to see what kind of reaction I'd get out of him. I didn't know what the hell the matter with me was, but the thought of him bringing home a woman for a romantic dinner bothered me. *Shit*. I wasn't even fond of Alex Parker.

It was 6:55. The candles were lit and the fresh red rose petals were laid perfectly around the table. I really went all out. As I was pouring two glasses of chardonnay, I heard the front door open, and my jaw dropped when Alex walked in with a guy.

Shit. Shit. Shit. His dinner guest wasn't a woman!

I stood there nervously, thinking about the dining room table I'd set.

"Emerson, this is Greyson Adair, CEO of Adair Holdings and Securities.

Greyson, this is my houseguest and chef, Emerson James."

Greyson looked at me as he took my hand and brought it up to his lips. "It's a pleasure to meet you."

"Thank you. It's nice to meet you."

"Is dinner ready?" Alex asked.

"Yes. I just have to plate it. Why don't the two of you go sit in the living room and have a drink? I'll call you when dinner is served. All I need is a few minutes," I spoke in a panic.

"There are two glasses of wine right there," Alex said as he reached for a glass.

"No!" I voiced as I took both glasses from the counter. "I mean, these are for dinner and must only be drunk with your meal. It's all about the pairing, Alex."

He gave me a strange look. A look that told me he knew I was up to something. But I didn't care. My only concern was getting the candles and rose petals off the table.

"Go on." I smiled as I waved my hands. "Go enjoy a pre-dinner drink."

He continued to stare at me as he led Greyson to the living room. When they were out of sight, I ran to the dining room, blew out the candles, grabbed them, and scooped up the rose petals, tossing them into the trash and hiding the candles in the cabinet. As I was plating their dinner, Alex and Greyson walked into the dining room and took a seat.

"Tonight's dinner is chicken scallopini with a shitake sake sauce over udon noodle cakes, steamed broccoli, and homemade dinner rolls, paired with a chardonnay." I smiled as I set down their plates in front of them.

"It smells like candles were blown out in here," Alex spoke as he raised his eyebrow at me. He leaned over his chair and picked up a single rose petal that must have fallen from my hands. "What's this?"

"It looks like a rose petal."

"I know what it looks like, Emerson. Where did it come from?"

I shrugged. "I don't know. Do you have roses around here somewhere?"

"No."

"Weird."

As I turned and began to walk away, Greyson called my name.

"Why don't you join us for dinner, Emerson?"

"Thank you. But I have to clean up and I've already eaten."

"Alex, tell your chef that she is required to join us."

I watched as Alex gave Greyson an odd look.

"Emerson, go get yourself a plate and sit down and join us for dinner," he spoke in an authoritative tone.

Flashing a fake smile, I went to the kitchen, made myself a plate, and sat down across from Alex.

"This chicken is amazing. May I ask where you learned to cook like this?" Greyson asked.

"I studied in Tuscany."

Alex's eyes focused on me when I said that.

"Under whom?" Greyson asked.

"Under Mario Ricci and his wife, Vanessa."

"Interesting," Alex spoke as he glared at me.

"Tuscany is a beautiful place. How long were you there?" Greyson continued with his questions.

"A little over six months."

"Well, this is extremely delicious and I must say I've never had udon noodle cakes before, but it's quickly becoming one of my favorites."

"Thank you." I smiled.

I sat and ate my dinner as the two of them talked business. I would be lying if I said that I wasn't turned on by Alex's business talk. I needed a smack upside the head.

Chapter 8

Alex

After finishing dinner and our business discussion, I escorted Greyson to the door, but not before he kissed Emerson on the cheek and thanked her for an enjoyable dinner. I didn't like the way he'd been staring at her. When he left, I followed her into the kitchen and watched as she put away the rest of the dishes.

"So you studied cooking in Tuscany?"

"Yep," she replied as she placed the plates in the cupboard.

"Why did you leave?"

"It was time to."

"Would you care to elaborate on that?" I asked.

She turned and looked at me as I sat down at the island with my hands folded on the granite countertop.

"Nope." She gave a small smile.

"Did you leave another broken heart behind?" I smirked.

"Maybe." She turned and reached up in the cupboard to put away the glasses.

There was a piece of plastic sitting on the counter, so I grabbed it and threw it in the trashcan. When I opened the lid, I noticed several red rose petals in the garbage.

"What are those?" I asked as I pointed to them.

She walked over and looked down into the garbage.

"Looks like rose petals. Strange. I wonder where they came from."

I cocked my head and glared at her. She knew damn well where they came from.

"Don't lie to me, Emerson. I don't like liars and I won't tolerate being lied to."

She rolled her eyes and put her hands up.

"Fine. You want the embarrassing truth? I thought your dinner guest was your girlfriend and I lit some candles and spread rose petals across the table to make the dinner more romantic. But when you walked in with Greyson, I freaked out and hurried and cleared the candles and the rose petals from the table. How would that have looked, having dinner with another man with candlelight and rose petals staring you in the face?"

I couldn't help but laugh. "First of all, I don't have a girlfriend and second of all, even if I did, she would have known something was wrong because I don't do candlelight dinners or rose petals."

Her left eye narrowed as she stared at me. "Why don't you do candlelight dinners or rose petals?"

"I don't know. Maybe I'm just not that romantic of a guy."

She shrugged and turned away. Turning back around, she narrowed her eye again. "If you don't have a girlfriend, who was that woman you were having lunch with the other day?"

"A casual friend whom I date on occasion."

Her eyes still narrowing at me, she spoke, "Ah, a friends-with-benefits type of woman. I gotcha."

"Friends with benefits?" I asked curiously.

"Yeah. You know. A person who you call a friend and have casual sex with. No strings, no commitments. Just sex, sex, and more sex when you want it."

She needed to stop saying the word "sex" because my cock was twitching uncontrollably and starting to get hard. The way the word "sex" rolled off her tongue turned me on. All I could picture was her bent over the island with her beautiful ass in the air while my cock was thrusting in and out of her, and her begging me to go deeper and faster. *Shit*. I needed to stop.

"Then I guess I have a lot of friends with benefits." I smiled.

"Good for you, Parker." She winked.

"How about you? Do you have any friends with benefits around the world?"

"I tried, but they always wanted more. It gets annoying after a while."

"I can relate," I spoke. "Well, I'm off to bed. Sleep tight."

"Breakfast will be on the table at 7:30 sharp. Don't you dare be a minute late or you can consider breakfast over."

I walked away, shaking my head with a small smile on my face. I found this woman more fascinating every day and I couldn't help but wonder what it would be like to kiss her beautiful, plump lips.

****

Emerson

At precisely 7:25 a.m., Alex walked into the kitchen, yelling at someone on the phone.

"Fuck that. If those plans aren't on my desk by the time I get into the office, you're fired. Do you understand? This is a multi-million-dollar deal and I won't lose it because you and your staff decided to play instead of doing your job. You'll all find yourselves out of jobs and I can guarantee that you'll never work in this state again. Am I making myself clear?" *Click.*

I placed his omelet on the plate as he walked into the dining room and took a seat.

"What a way to start your day. Good morning."

"Don't get smart with me, Emerson. I'm in no mood."

Was he serious? How the hell was I getting smart with him? I wanted to throw the plate at him and watch the omelet slide down and stain his expensive, but sexy as fuck, designer suit. Instead, I nicely set it down in front of him.

"Are you eating?" he asked with an attitude.

"I already ate. Enjoy your omelet." I walked out of the dining room and back into the kitchen to clean up.

"Emerson, I need more coffee," he yelled from the other room.

I rolled my eyes and looked at Jenna, who had just arrived at the house. I took the carafe from the cupboard and filled it with the rest of the coffee from the pot. Walking into the dining room, I set it on the table.

"There. Now you can pour your own coffee without having to yell for me to get it for you."

"You better watch that attitude of yours, Miss James."

I took a bow in front of him. "I'm sorry, Your Majesty. It'll never happen again." I walked away and heard him mumble.

As I entered the kitchen, Jenna was laughing.

"I can't believe you just did that. Nobody speaks to Mr. Parker that way."

"Why is everyone so afraid of him?" I asked as I sipped on my coffee.

"Because he's Alex Parker. That's why."

"He's a human being just like everyone else, and if he chooses to live life like an asshole, then that's his problem. Life's too short to live like that."

"Are you going to be the one to tell him that?" she asked with a smile.

"If I have to, then yes."

"Good luck. It was nice knowing you." She lightly touched my arm and walked away.

I was starting to feel suffocated in this house and I needed to get out and do things. I was used to keeping busy. Coming and going as I pleased, and without a vehicle here in California, it was impossible. Phillip couldn't be at my beck and call whenever I needed to go somewhere, so I had to find a solution to my problem. I grabbed my phone from the counter and dialed Adam.

"Hello, Emerson. How are things going?"

"I'm suffocating here and I need to borrow your car while you're gone."

There was silence on the other end.

"Hello. Did you hear me? Can I please borrow your car?"

Again, a moment of silence and then a sigh. "I guess. But you better be careful with it."

"Thank you, Adam, and I promise I will be. Is it at your house?"

"Yep. It's in the garage. The keys are in the drawer to the left of the stove. The contractors are there, working, so you should be able to get in. I can't stress enough about my car, Em. You better take good care of it."

"I will."

"How's it going with Alex?"

"He's a pompous, uptight, pain in the ass."

He snickered. "Sounds like Alex. Are you behaving yourself?"

"Of course. I'm on my best behavior in front of His Majesty."

"God, Em. That right there tells me things aren't going so well."

"You worry too much. Go back to work and thanks for the car. I love you!" *Click.*

I sent a text message to Phillip.

"Can you drive me to my brother's house, please?"

"When do you need to go?"

"As soon as possible."

"I'll be there in about fifteen minutes."

"Thank you, Phillip."

Chapter 9

Alex

In and out of meetings all day, dealing with ignorant people, a mess of problems, and thinking about Emerson left me exhausted. I wasn't feeling well, so I decided to call it a night and go home. As Phillip pulled up to the house, I noticed Adam's car in the driveway.

"Phillip, do you know why Adam's car is here?"

"I drove Emerson to his house today to pick it up. She told me she'll be driving herself around from now on."

"I see." I climbed out of the Bentley and told him to have a good night.

After I walked upstairs to my bedroom, I changed into my swimsuit and decided to go for a swim. Besides sex, a good swim always relieved some tension. As I stepped out onto the patio, I saw Emerson in the pool. I sighed because I wasn't in any mood to deal with her tonight.

"Hey. You're home early tonight."

"Yeah. I just need to go for a swim before I do some work from home."

She climbed out of the pool, looking as sexy as fuck. "It's all yours." She smiled.

"You didn't have to get out."

"It's fine. I was done anyway. I'm just going to sit here and have some wine."

After doing a couple of laps, I started to feel relaxed. I got out, dried myself off, and took a seat in the lounge chair next to Emerson.

"I saw Adam's car in the driveway. Phillip told me he drove you to his house today to get it."

"I need a car to get around. I have things to do and it's too difficult to depend on Phillip to take me places."

"Things?" I asked curiously.

"Life things." She smiled.

I took in a deep breath and placed my hand on my head. I had a really bad headache and the only thing I could think about was going to bed and sleeping it off.

"Are you okay?" Emerson asked.

"I just have a really bad headache. I think it's one of the worst ones I've ever had. I'm going to call it a night and go lie down."

"Here, let me help you," she spoke as she got up from her chair and stepped behind me, placing her hands on my head.

"What are you doing?"

"I'm giving you a head massage with a special technique I learned in Thailand."

She began rubbing my head, and instantly, I started to get hard. *Shit.* I rested my hands over my growing bulge.

"Thailand, eh?"

"Yes. Now be quiet, close your eyes, and relax."

Easy for her to say. She wasn't the one getting turned on and hard. I closed my eyes and did my best to relax. It was difficult with her hands on me. I'd had many massages and I'd never once become hard because of them. This was crazy and I was going to have to go and jack off once she was finished or I was going to have a serious case of blue balls.

The tips of her fingers massaged my temples in a way I'd never felt before. Her hands roamed from my temples to my forehead and then over my entire head, massaging in circles and pressing down with her thumbs. I was in heaven and it was taking everything I had in me not to turn around, grab her, and kiss that sassy mouth of hers.

"Tell me about Thailand," I spoke, trying to get my cock to go down.

"It was beautiful."

"How long were you there?"

"About six months. I learned this special massage technique from a healer there. I wasn't feeling well and had collapsed outside of the hotel I was staying at. He and his wife were walking past and helped me. They took me to their home and I ended up staying with them as their guest until I left. He taught me various healing techniques and his wife and I cooked together. She taught me some things and I taught her things I learned in Tuscany. They were very nice people."

"Why did you leave?"

"As beautiful as it was, my time there was up and I needed to move on. Now no more questions. I'm almost done."

I took in a deep breath as she continued to work her magic on my headache. How in the world could she have traveled so much at her age, and not to mention the fact that she traveled alone, which was unsafe and dangerous for a young woman.

She removed her hands from my head and gripped my shoulders. "There. How do you feel?"

"Wow. My headache is gone." I turned and looked at her.

"Good." She winked as she removed her hands from my shoulders.

Without even thinking, I grabbed her hand. "Thank you," I spoke as I stared into her eyes.

"You're welcome. It's the least I could do since you're letting me stay here and you're letting me cook for you. That right there is an honor."

That smart sarcastic mouth of hers was going to get her in trouble with me. I let go of her hand and she jumped in the pool.

"Would you like to race?" she asked with a smile.

Staring at her as the water glistened on her tan skin, I got up and jumped in.

"You're on, James."

"First one to make it back here has to cook breakfast in the morning," she said with a whimsical tone.

"I don't cook."

"You will tomorrow if I win. Ready…set…go!"

We did a full lap to the other side of the pool and turned around and headed back. She was fast and ahead of me. She made it to the other side first. When I came up, she was grinning from ear to ear.

"Are you some kind of fucking swimming champion I don't know about?"

She bit down on her bottom lip and my cock twitched.

"Maybe just a national champion for my school."

"Jesus, Emerson. You couldn't have told me that?"

"Then it wouldn't have been fun. Looks like you're cooking breakfast tomorrow!" she exclaimed.

As she started to climb out of the pool, I grabbed her waist and pulled her down into my arms. *What the fuck am I doing?* She wrapped her arms around my neck and stared at me.

"I already told you that I don't cook."

"A bet is a bet."

"You made the bet. I didn't agree to it." I stared at her lips. She wasn't pulling away from me. *Control yourself, Alex. She's not your type and you'll end up hurting her and making things awkward between you and Adam.*

I let go of her. "I'm going to head to bed. I'll see you in the morning." I climbed out of the pool, grabbed my towel, and went inside the house.

****

Emerson

I sighed as I watched him walk away. He wanted to kiss me. I could tell by the way he was staring at my mouth. Not to mention the fact that I noticed he was hard as I was massaging his head. If he would have kissed me, I wouldn't have minded. There was a part of me that would have welcomed it. He was unlike anyone I'd ever met before and, for some dumb reason, I was attracted to him in a weird sort of way.

I dried myself off, and as I headed to my bedroom, Alex was walking up the stairs.

"Goodnight, Alex," I spoke.

Chapter 10

Alex

I stopped on the stairs and clenched my fists. “Emerson,” I called out to her.

“Yes.” She stood in front of the stairs, looking up at me.

I slowly walked down until I approached her. “I don’t want you walking around this house in your bikini or short shorts anymore. Do you understand me?”

“No, actually, I don’t. What’s wrong?”

I took in a deep breath. “It’s inappropriate.”

“So do you want me to walk around naked?” She smirked.

“No. I don’t want you to walk around naked. What the hell is the matter with you? Why would you say that?”

“Because, obviously, my clothes bother you.”

“Emerson, I’m warning you. I’ve had enough of that smart mouth of yours and if you don’t stop, I’m going to shut it for you.”

She looked at me with narrowing eyes and a small smile on her face. “I dare you.”

That was it. I lost control as I grabbed her face and smashed my mouth into hers, forcing her lips to part as my tongue entered her mouth. She placed her hands on the back of my neck as our kiss deepened. She wanted me to kiss her. Her soft lips had me hard and wanting to be inside her. I couldn't control myself and I had to have her. Especially after that massage she gave me. I lifted her up as she wrapped her legs around me and carried her to her bedroom. Laying her on the bed, my hands groped her luscious round breasts as my mouth continued to devour hers.

"Do you want me to fuck you, Emerson?"

"Yes."

"Say it," I commanded.

"I want you to fuck me, Alex."

"I can promise you that it won't be soft and gentle. I like it hard and fast and I'm always in control."

"I wouldn't expect anything else from you. But you better satisfy me, Parker, because if you don't, I'm going to be pissed off."

How dare she. I sat up and took down her bottoms, revealing her beautifully shaven pussy. It was more beautiful than I had imagined it would be and I needed to taste her. When I placed my tongue on her clit, she threw her head back and let out a moan, sending me into a frenzy. I dipped two fingers inside her and moved them around as my tongue licked around her.

"Untie your bikini top and show me your tits," I commanded.

She reached behind her as my fingers explored her and untied her top, letting it fall forward, exposing her breasts. Her nipples peaked with excitement and were the perfect rosy color I thought they'd be. I moved up her, my fingers still inside, and took her nipple in my mouth, lightly nipping at it and then licking to soothe the sting. She was losing control as she moaned and her body tightened, giving in to the orgasm I gave her. Standing up, I took off my bathing suit and climbed on top of her. As my cock was at her entrance, I stopped.

"Fuck. I need to go get a condom."

"Don't you dare ruin this moment. I'm on birth control."

"Any STDs?" I asked.

"No. You?"

"Absolutely not."

"Then what are you waiting for?" She smiled.

Without hesitation, I thrust inside her, hard and deep. I wanted to fuck her a million different ways. After a few thrusts, I pulled out and flipped her over, taking her from behind. The warmth that radiated inside her enveloped my cock, making it difficult for me to hold back. As I slammed into her at a rapid pace, she orgasmed. I moaned loudly as the buildup began. One last thrust and I pulled out of her, spilling my come all over her back and beautifully sculpted ass.

I climbed off of her and lay on my back, trying to catch my breath as she stared at me.

"Why did you pull out?" she asked breathlessly.

"Because I really don't know if you're on birth control or not."

She didn't say a word. The only thing she did was turn her head and look the other way. I got up from the bed, grabbed some tissues from the nightstand, and wiped Emerson's backside. I leaned down and softly kissed her shoulder.

"Listen, I'm sorry. But I barely know you and I shouldn't have let this happen."

She turned her head and looked at me. "We both wanted it, Alex. It's no big deal, so don't get all bent out of shape over it."

"You're Adam's sister."

"So what? He never has to know. If you'll excuse me, I'm going to take a shower." She climbed off the bed and walked to the bathroom.

I picked up my bathing suit from the floor and went upstairs to my bedroom. It wasn't like me to lose control like that. Emerson James had done something to me. Something that I couldn't explain.

****

Emerson

His scent still lingered throughout my room. He didn't trust me when I said I was on birth control and that pissed me off. I shouldn't have let that bother me. If he didn't trust me, that was his problem, not mine. I was a young woman and I needed sex. I could tell he wanted me, so I let him have me. That way, we both got what we wanted. To say he was amazing would be an understatement. He was strong and the way he brought me to two orgasms was incredible. Half the time, I had to fake it with the other guys I slept with. They were lucky if they could manage to bring me to have one. But with Alex, it happened flawlessly, and for that, I was grateful. I could tell he had regrets, but I didn't, at least not at this moment. Would this change things between us? No. He would still be the same pompous ass he was when I first met him.

The next morning, I got up, dressed, went down to the kitchen, and started a pot of coffee. I popped a banana-nut muffin in the microwave. As I was about to eat it, Alex walked in.

"Good morning. Is breakfast ready?" he asked as he poured himself a cup of coffee.

"No. You were supposed to cook breakfast this morning," I replied as I bit into my muffin.

"You're kidding me, right?" He stared blankly at me.

"Nope. I won. You lost and the loser had to cook breakfast."

"We went over this last night, Emerson, and I told you that I don't cook."

"Then I guess you can have a muffin." I smiled.

He mumbled as he took a muffin from the counter and took his coffee into the dining room. He looked really pissed, but I didn't care. I went to my room and took my birth control pills from the nightstand. Walking into the dining room, I threw them on the table.

"You can see for yourself that I wasn't lying." I walked away.

A few moments later, he threw my pills on the island and left the house without saying a word.

Over the next few days, I barely saw him. I kept myself busy by meeting up with Christine and Bayli. The only time I really saw Alex was when I made his breakfast. I loved to cook, so I didn't mind. The only words we had spoken to each other were "good morning." I guess he was still holding a grudge against me for not making his breakfast the other morning. He was a big boy and he'd get over it sooner or later. When he'd come strolling in around eleven o'clock in the evening, he'd go straight up to his room. It bothered me a bit that since we'd had sex, he'd barely spoken to me. But this situation was only temporary, because as soon as Adam came back, I would leave and then I wouldn't have to worry about Alex Parker ever again. Even if he did leave an imprint on me.

Chapter 11

Emerson

After going for a late-night swim, I grabbed a bottle of water from the refrigerator. As I was walking through the living room, I saw Alex lying on the couch. I didn't even know he was home.

"Are you okay?" I stopped and asked.

"I'm fine. Just go to bed, Emerson," he spoke in his annoying, commanding voice.

"Are you sure? You don't look too well."

"I said I'm fine. It was a long day and I'm tired."

"Okay. Good night." I walked away and he didn't say a word.

When I got up the next morning at six a.m., I noticed Alex was still on the couch, asleep. I made a pot of coffee and went to my bedroom to get dressed. When I came back out, I saw him sitting up. He looked as pale as a ghost.

"Are you okay?" I asked in a panic.

"I don't know. My heart is racing, my head is killing me, and my vision is blurry."

"Are you having chest pains?"

"A little bit."

"I'm taking you to the hospital, Alex."

"NO! I'll be fine in a few minutes."

"Not up for discussion, you stubborn ass."

I ran up the stairs and opened the door to what I thought was his bedroom, but ended up being his office. I closed the door and opened the one further down the hall. Holy shit! His bedroom was huge! I'd never seen anything like it. Going over to the dresser, I opened all his drawers until I found a pair of sweatpants and a t-shirt. I ran down the stairs to him.

"Here. You need to get dressed," I spoke as I pulled the t-shirt over his head.

"Did you go through my things?" he angrily asked.

"Yes, I did. Now shut the hell up and help me put on your pants. You could be having a stroke or a heart attack."

He didn't say a word as I helped him up from the couch, grabbed my purse, and helped him to Adam's car. Opening the passenger door, I told him to get in. I drove to the hospital as fast as I could. Maybe I should have called an ambulance, but I could get him there faster. Weaving in and out of traffic, laying on the horn at stupid people who didn't know how to drive, and checking on him every second I could, I pulled up to the emergency room and yelled for help. Two nurses came running out with a wheelchair and took him inside. I followed behind.

"Excuse me, but are you his wife?"

"No."

"Then you're going to have to wait in the waiting room. We'll call you in as soon as we can."

I rolled my eyes and took a seat in the waiting room. I didn't have time to think about my reaction to being here until after Alex was taken away. My focus was on getting him here before he possibly keeled over and died. With shaking hands, I grabbed a cup of coffee from the lousy coffee machine in the waiting room and attempted to drink it without spilling it all over my clothes. I paced back and forth, watching the people who were here with loved ones stare at me with sadness in their eyes.

"For Alex Parker?" A nurse walked into the room.

"Yes."

"You can follow me."

She led me down the hall and to the room where Alex was lying in a bed. He looked pissed as hell when I walked into the room.

"You may stay until the doctor comes in," the nurse spoke.

The room, the faint beep of the machine that Alex was hooked up to, and the smell were bringing back so many memories. Memories that sent me straight into a panic attack.

"Emerson, are you okay?" Alex asked.

I couldn't breathe and my heart was racing a mile a minute.

"Emerson!" Alex yelled. I couldn't answer him. He yelled for the nurse and she came running in, took one look at me, and led me over to the window.

"See that tree outside? Stare at it and breathe. Focus on nothing else. That tree is your focal point," she spoke as she lightly held on to my arm.

My breathing was returning to normal and I was coming out of my attack.

"There you go, honey. Sit down in this chair and relax for a minute."

I looked at Alex, who had a pained look on his face.

"Do you normally have panic attacks?" the nurse asked.

"I used to. But it's been several years."

"Do you know what set it off?"

I slowly nodded my head. "This place."

"I'm going to get you some water. Sit tight."

She left the room and I once again looked at Alex.

"What the hell just happened?" he asked.

"I can ask you the same thing," I replied.

A man walked in and introduced himself as Dr. Malone.

"Are you his wife?" he asked.

Why the hell does everyone keep asking me that? "No. I'm his houseguest."

"Then I'm going to have to ask you to step out of the room."

I looked over at Alex. "I'll call Phillip to come pick you up." I got up from my seat and walked out, practically running out like hell. I pulled my phone from my purse and took a seat outside on the bench.

"Phillip, it's Emerson. I took Mr. Parker to the ER and I need you to pick him up."

"Is he okay?"

"I think so."

"I'm on my way."

I got into my car and gripped the steering wheel until my knuckles turned white as I stared at the hospital building. The last place I wanted to go was back to Alex's house, so I drove to the one place that held many special memories for me.

****

Sitting in the sand on Venice Beach, I watched as the surfers surfed, the kids played in the water, and the teenagers who skipped school hung out and had some fun.

"Can you believe I'm back here, Emily? It's been so long. The nightmares are back and I had my first panic attack today in eight years. It's this place and the trauma of what happened here."

I looked over at two little girls who were building a sand castle and smiled as tears sprang to my eyes. Pain filled my heart as I thought of my sister. I was living my life for her. Doing all the things we talked about since we were kids. I took my phone from my purse. It was already five o'clock. Feelings of guilt crept over me for leaving Alex the way I did. Getting up from the sand, I dusted myself off and drove back to his house.

When I walked through the door, Jenna was just getting ready to leave for the day.

"Where have you been?" she asked in a whisper.

"Is he home?"

"Yes. He's upstairs resting. I wouldn't go up there if I were you. He's in a foul mood."

"What else is new? I'll just wait until he comes down."

I made myself a sandwich and took it outside on the patio with a bottle of wine. Finishing up my sandwich, I took my glass and the bottle down to the beach. As I was sipping on my wine, I heard Alex's voice behind me.

"It's about time you came home. Where have you been all day?"

"How are you feeling?" I asked as I turned around and looked at him. He was shirtless and wearing the pair of sweatpants I had helped him into earlier.

"Answer my question," he commanded as he sat down next to me.

"Answer *my* question."

"I asked you first," he spoke as he took the glass from my hand and took a drink.

"Where I was doesn't matter. What matters right now is how you're feeling. Should you even be out of bed?"

He sighed as he handed me back my glass.

"It's okay. You keep it. I have the whole bottle." I smiled as I held it up.

"I have high blood pressure and, right now, I'm feeling a lot better."

"I'm not surprised."

"You're not?" He arched his brow.

"No. You keep long hours, you yell a lot, and you get upset when you feel like you're losing control. To be honest, you're a heart attack waiting to happen."

He laughed. "Thanks. So are you going to tell me about that panic attack you had at the hospital?"

Chapter 12

Emerson

Now he wanted to talk to me? After all the days that went by and he couldn't be bothered?

"It's being back here. I never should have let Adam talk me into coming back."

He looked at me in confusion. "I don't understand."

"You know, with the accident and stuff."

"What accident?"

"Didn't Adam tell you?" I frowned.

"Tell me what? I didn't even know he had a sister until he asked if you could stay with me."

I rolled my eyes. "Of course he didn't tell you."

"I'll be honest with you. I don't know anything about Adam's personal life. He has never talked about his family or anything. The only thing I knew was about a girl he had dated for a while."

"Really? I always thought he was gay." I smirked.

Alex chuckled. It was good to see him laugh. I took in a deep breath and took a sip of wine from the bottle.

"When I was sixteen years old, I was in a bad car accident with my parents and my identical twin sister, Emily. They were killed and I spent three months in that hospital in a coma. I actually had died for a couple of minutes, but the doctors were able to bring me back. There were times that I wished they hadn't." I lowered my head and looked down at the sand.

"Emerson, don't say that," Alex whispered as he reached over and placed his hand on mine.

I pulled away because I didn't want or need his pity. He was lucky I was even telling him everything. Bringing the bottle of wine up to my lips, I took another sip.

"When I woke up from the coma, Adam told me everyone was dead. I felt like my soul was gone and I wanted to die. I couldn't believe they were gone. Emily was my best friend in the whole world and we did everything together. When she died, a huge piece of me died with her."

I got up from the sand and walked towards the water, Alex following behind.

"Besides the coma, a couple of bruises, and a fractured knee, I lost complete control in my right arm due to severe nerve damage. After surgery, I spent a year in rehab, trying to regain use of it again. The doctors said I only had a twenty percent chance of it ever fully recovering and that I needed to get used to doing things with one arm."

"But you did recover," Alex softly spoke as we walked along the water.

"I did because of Emily. Swimming was our life and we trained in the pool every day since we were seven years old. Our parents didn't know we were training; they only knew how much we loved the water. Emily had her heart set on becoming an Olympic swimmer. She wanted nothing more than to make the USA Olympic team. My goal wasn't that big. But I trained with her anyway because it meant so much to her. Before the accident happened, she was training for the national swim meet for our high school. She was on her way to the top and everyone had their eye on her."

"What about you?"

"I was on the team too, but it was her dream. Not mine. So I pulled back to let her have the spotlight."

"That was very admirable of you." He smiled.

"Thanks. There was nothing we wouldn't do for each other."

I stopped walking and stared out into the ocean. Alex stopped beside me and brushed a strand of my hair from my face. I took his hand and held it.

"I'm so sorry for leaving you at the hospital."

"Please, don't apologize. You have nothing to be sorry for. I completely understand why you had to get out of there."

I let go of his hand as I gave him a small smile.

"So how did you become a national swim champion?" he asked.

"Since it was Emily's dream, I decided that I was going to try and win it for her. Rehab helped. They exercised my arm to try and rebuild my strength in it. I swam every single day, sometimes for four to five hours and practiced only using one arm. The coach didn't want to let me back on the team at first because she didn't think I would be a good asset with only being able to use one arm. But I showed her. I got into that pool and swam my heart out, beating out my teammates who could swim with both arms. Our team made it to the nationals and suddenly I wasn't sure if I could do it. Anxiety started to set in because I was so afraid of letting Emily down. Doubt started to fill my mind and I began to question why I was even there. I remember sitting in the locker room on the bench. The rest of the team had already headed to the pool. I begged Emily to give me the strength to go through with it. I met my team out on the benches by the pool and, all of a sudden, a white dove came out of nowhere and landed by me. I knew that was the sign from Emily. I swam that day like I never swam before, breaking three national records."

Alex took hold of both my hands, bringing them up to his lips. "Congratulations. I'm very proud of you."

"Thank you."

****

Alex

Listening to her story was heartbreaking, yet fulfilling. Emerson James was a phenomenal woman and, apparently, I didn't give her enough credit. I had no clue that she had lost her parents and twin sister and my heart ached for her. My heart never ached for anything or anyone. But for her, it did.

"So after Nationals, what did you do?" I asked as I continued to hold her hands.

"After high school, I packed up and left California. This is the first time I've been back since I was eighteen years old."

"I'm surprised colleges didn't offer you scholarships."

"They did." She smiled. "I didn't want to go to college. As much as I loved to swim, it wasn't my dream. I only did it for Emily. I had other plans. I wanted to travel the world just like me and Emily planned to do."

"I'm surprised Adam let you."

I laughed. "He didn't have a choice, plus I had already been a burden on him since the accident. He was still in college and had to take care of me. That wasn't in his life plan and I hated that he put his life on hold for me."

"How did you have the money to travel?" I asked out of curiosity.

"My parents were wealthy. Not like you wealthy. But they led a comfortable life. After they were killed, Adam sold our childhood home. Between that money and all the investments that my parents had and their savings, we had a lot of money to split between us. The only way Adam agreed to me traveling was if he kept control of my finances, since that was his specialty. I agreed and then left. When I was running low on money, I would call him and he would send some more."

"Did you ever work?"

"Yeah. I took on odd jobs here and there. When I was in Texas, I worked at Billy's ranch, taking care of the horses. That's how we met."

"Why did you leave Texas?"

"I had been there just under six months and it was time to move on to the next adventure."

"I still don't understand why you had to come back to California."

"Apparently, my money is almost gone, which I can't understand since I was very careful, and Adam said that I need to settle down in one place. He wouldn't send me any more money until after we talked. So, I'm waiting for him to come back so we can have our conversation and I can get on with my life. Are you hungry?"

"Yeah. Actually, I am." I smiled.

"Then let's go cook some dinner. There's a couple of steaks in the refrigerator."

"Sounds good. You can cook and I'll get another bottle of wine ready." I winked.

As we headed up to the house, I couldn't help but think how much her life had changed in the blink of an eye. She was such a beautiful and courageous woman and she had touched my life like no one ever had before. I was starting to see things differently through her eyes and, to be honest, it scared me.

Chapter 13

Emerson

After seasoning the steaks, I threw them on the grill and started to cut up some vegetables.

"So where are you off to next?" he asked.

"I don't know. I'll have to look at my map."

"Your map?" His brow arched.

I told him that I'd be right back and I went to my room and took my map from underneath the bed. Bringing it back to the kitchen, I laid it out on the counter.

"See these red circles? Those are the places I already visited. The ones in black are where I still have to go."

"You and your sister did this?"

"Yep. We had been working on this map since we were ten years old, circling all the places we were going to visit. It hung on our bedroom wall and whenever we had an idea or thought of a place, we'd circle it on the map."

He looked at me and smiled. "That was a great idea the two of you had, but I still don't understand why you have to visit all these places now. Why not spread them over your lifetime?"

"Because, Alex, you never know when your time is going to be up. Never stay in one place too long. There's too much beauty in the world to see."

"Well, it looks like you're going to have to slow down since your money is running out," he spoke as he poured the wine.

"I'll find a way." I smiled.

I made the salad and took the steaks off the grill. Alex shocked me by setting the table on the patio.

"I didn't think you knew how to set the table."

"I'm not that incapable of things. I do run a multi-billion-dollar company, after all."

He still was in his sweatpants and no shirt. Staring at his rock hard chest and eight pack was getting to be unbearable. The ache between my legs was getting out of control knowing what the man could do to me.

"I think what you're wearing is inappropriate and you should go change."

He gave me a blank stare. "What?"

"You have no shirt on and it's inappropriate. Please go put on a shirt before we sit down and eat."

The corners of his mouth curved up as he walked over to me and ran his thumb across my lips.

"You didn't seem to be complaining when I was on top of you totally naked."

I gulped as I remembered that night and the things he did to me.

"That was different. We were having sex. We're not having sex now, so please go and clothe yourself."

"Fine. I will. But don't be surprised if later, the clothes come off." He winked and walked away.

My stomach fluttered at the thought. I set dinner on the patio and a few moments later, Alex walked out wearing a pair of khaki shorts and a short-sleeve polo shirt.

"Better?" he asked as he held out his hands.

"Yes. Much better."

As he sat down at the table, he looked around. "Where's the salt?"

"No salt. It's bad for your blood pressure. Starting today, I'm going to make sure you eat properly."

"Shit. I love salt."

"You'll learn to live without it. So, since I told you my life story, I want to hear all about Alex Parker. How the hell did you become a billionaire by the age of thirty?"

"How did you know how old I was?"

"I googled you."

He raised his eyebrow and gave a small smile. "Why?"

"Because I needed to find out who the stranger was that my brother was sending me to stay with. And by the way? What sort of brother does that?"

"He obviously trusts me." He chuckled.

"Big mistake on his part." I smiled.

"Apparently, after what happened the other night."

I laughed. "Go on, tell me about yourself."

"I came from money. My grandfather started the company, my father took over when he died, and I did the same when my father passed away."

"I'm sorry. I didn't know he passed. How long ago?"

"It's been about five years."

"And what about your mom?"

"She and my father divorced when I was seventeen and I haven't seen her since. She moved to Hawaii."

"Oh nice. I mean, not nice for you, but Hawaii is nice. I was there for about four months. I loved it."

"Of course you were," he spoke as he ate his steak.

"May I ask why you haven't seen her?"

"She was the reason they got divorced. She had met someone else and left him. I don't like the guy she's with, so I never bothered to keep in touch with her. She didn't even have the decency to come to my father's funeral."

"I'm sorry."

"Nah, don't be."

I could hear the pain that resided in his voice as he spoke about her.

"So you inherited the company. Were you ready to take over?"

"I sure was. The board didn't think so and they thought it would be best if I waited a few more years, but I stood my ground and showed them that I could take the company further. That's when I invested in some hotels, made a national chain, and made the company billions."

I held up my wine glass to him. "Congratulations. I'm very proud of you."

He tipped his glass to mine. "Thank you, Miss James."

"Tell me what you do for fun. Because since I've been here, you don't do anything but work."

"I have sex with beautiful women. That's what I do for fun." He smirked.

Ouch. For some reason, that stung. The thought of him being with other women sent a fire burning through my veins.

"Besides sex, you nympho. Do you have any hobbies?"

"I golf."

"Of course you do."

"What's that supposed to mean?" He glared at me.

"You're a corporate billionaire and they all golf. I bet you conduct business on the golf course too."

"And what if I did."

"Ha!" I pointed at him. "I knew it. Typical corporate man!"

"I don't appreciate being stereotyped like that."

I rolled my eyes. "Then step out of the 'corporate man' stereotype and do something different."

"Like what?"

"I don't know. Think about it and get back to me."

He chuckled. "Okay. Because I have time to do that."

My light and fluffy mood changed to seriousness. "Alex, I'm serious. You had a health scare today and you need to slow down. You're so fucking filthy rich that you're set for life. You don't need to keep going at the rate you are. Life is too short to live that way. You need to let go and discover who you are outside of the corporate world. Relax and have some fun."

"You mean become irresponsible with life like you? No thanks."

Fuck. Did he really just say that? It was nice to know what he really thought of me.

"I'm not irresponsible, Alex."

He laughed. "Come on, Emerson. Yes you are. You travel around the world without any care or responsibility. You don't take life seriously. Isn't that why Adam forced you to come back here? So he can put an end to this irresponsible life you're living?"

Burn. Burn. Burn. Who the fuck did he think he was?

I set down my fork, took the napkin from my lap, threw it on my plate, and pointed my finger at him.

"This is my life and nobody tells me how to live it. I have no regrets with how I've lived because I've been to hell and back a thousand times over! So you can take your irresponsible words and shove them up your ass, Parker." I turned on my heels and stormed into the house, going to my bedroom, locking the door, and throwing myself on my bed. I refused to cry.

Chapter 14

Alex

Did she really just tell me to shove my irresponsible words up my ass? I sat there shaking my head. I didn't say anything that wasn't the truth, and the fact that she got so pissed off by it showed that she knew it was true. I sighed as I got up from my chair and cleared the table. Seeing her so upset by what I said was starting to bother me, so I went to her room and knocked on the door.

"Emerson, let's talk, please."

She didn't respond.

I turned the knob, only to find it was locked. "Emerson, open this door! This is my fucking house," I yelled.

Suddenly, the door opened. "Stop yelling. I bet your blood pressure is sky high right now."

"You make me yell," I spoke as I stepped inside the room.

Walking over to her, I placed my hands on her shoulders. She pushed away from me.

"Don't touch me."

"You don't really mean that," I spoke as I placed my hand on her cheek.

"Yes I do." She looked down but didn't pull away.

"I'm sorry if I sounded harsh. Sometimes, things just fly out of my mouth."

"I know and it's annoying."

I smiled as I lifted her chin and softly brushed my lips against hers.

"Do you forgive me?"

"No."

"Is there anything I can do to make you forgive me?" I smiled softly as my hand traveled up her shirt and over her breast, pulling down the cup of her bra and taking her nipple between my fingers.

"No." I saw a small smile escape her lips.

"Are you sure?" I took her hand and placed it on my hard cock.

"Yes."

"Yes you're sure or yes you want this?"

"I'm sure."

I unbuttoned her shorts and took them down along with her panties. I kneeled down, and my mouth tasted her. She was wet and I knew damn well she wanted me. She moaned as I plunged a finger inside her.

"Still sure?" I whispered.

"Damn you, Parker." She placed her hands on my head as my tongue explored her. I smiled as I stood up and lifted her shirt over her head. Unhooking her bra, I tossed it to the floor and let my mouth devour her beautiful breasts.

I lightly pushed her back on the bed and hovered over her as she moaned to the pleasure I was giving her. The sweet sounds that escaped her turned me on and I couldn't become any harder than I already was. She threw her head back and let out a soft cry when I inserted another finger and sent her into ecstasy as she orgasmed. Standing up, I stripped out of my clothes and lay down next to her, wrapping my arms around her and pulling her on her side so she was facing me.

Brushing a strand of hair from her face, I softly kissed her mouth as my cock slowly thrust inside her. We gasped at the pleasure as she tilted her head and my lips explored her neck. She wrapped her leg around my waist, forcing me to deepen inside her. Grabbing hold of her breast, I sped up and moved in and out of her swiftly. Her pussy swelled over my cock, causing it to tingle with delight and making me want to come. But I had to hold back. This wasn't going to be over so soon. I slowed down the pace and we stared into each other's eyes. Reaching down, I rubbed her swollen clit until she couldn't take anymore and she released herself to me. Rolling on top of her, I didn't want to hold back anymore. I pounded into her, fast and hard, giving her everything I had. I halted as I pushed one last time, burying myself deep inside her as I filled her with my come. Collapsing on top of her, I held her tightly and kissed the side of her neck as her arms tightened themselves around me. I pulled out of her and rolled onto my back.

"Am I forgiven?" I asked with a smile.

"Maybe." She smirked.

I climbed off the bed and grabbed some tissues from the nightstand. She got up, pulled back the sheets, climbed in, and held them up to me. I climbed in next to her and wrapped my arms around her as she snuggled into me, lightly running her fingers up and down my arm.

"Why do you break so many hearts?" I asked.

"Relationships are fun as long as they don't get too serious, and the guys I dated got too serious. Which I found weird because it's usually the girls who become so attached. I can't even settle down in life, let alone settle down with one guy. What about you? Why have you broken so many hearts?"

"I guess you could say I think the same way you do, but I'm settled in my life with a home and my company."

She turned on her side and propped herself up on her elbow. "Since you're settled, don't you want to settle down and have a family?"

"I never really gave it much thought. I like dating different women and it just seems silly to settle down with one for the rest of your life. I mean, look at how my parents turned out."

"True, I guess. My parents were so in love that it was quite embarrassing sometimes."

"Growing up with that didn't make you want to settle down with someone special?" I asked as I ran my finger across her forehead.

She looked down and began playing with the bed sheet. "Maybe it did once. But since the accident, my views on life changed."

"What about Adam? How did he handle everything?"

"He doesn't talk about it. He never did. All he would say was, 'They're gone and we need to move on.' So I did and he disapproves."

"How often did you see him if you haven't been back here in eight years?"

"We talked on the phone a few times a week and I usually saw him at Christmas. But he would come to wherever I was."

"I don't mean to upset you by reliving the past, but where was Adam when the accident happened?"

"He was away at college. My parents were taking me and my sister to the ballet and it was raining something awful outside. My dad could barely see the road and my mom kept telling him to pull over. He said if he pulled over, we were going to be late and he didn't want to disappoint his girls. We were coming around a curve and the last thing I remember was my mom screaming, 'Look out,' and the car rolling over several times before hitting a tree and stopping. I remember grabbing Emily's hand and squeezing it tight. Then everything went black except I could still hear voices in the distance. As the voices got closer, I heard a man say, 'This one is still alive.' After that, I don't remember a thing except waking up in the hospital three months later."

"I'm so sorry, Emerson," I softly spoke as I stroked her cheek. "Is that what your nightmare was about?"

"Yeah. After the accident, I had them just about every night. But once I left California, they stopped. Now that I'm back, so are they, but not as frequent as they were. I'm going to go to sleep now."

I kissed her forehead before she snuggled against me and I wrapped my arms tightly around her. I wanted her to feel safe and I wanted her to sleep in peace.

Chapter 15

Emerson

When I opened my eyes, I was alone. I glanced over at the clock and it was six-thirty. *Shit.* Where was Alex? I needed to get up and start breakfast. Climbing out of bed, I noticed a piece of paper propped up on the dresser. Walking over to it, I picked it up and discovered it was from Alex.

Emerson,

No need to worry about breakfast this morning. I needed to get into the office early since I wasn't there yesterday. I didn't want to wake you. See you later.

Alex

At least he didn't want to wake me, but I wouldn't have minded if he had. Something happened last night between us. There was a connection. I had never told any of the guys I dated about the accident, my parents, or sister. There was no need for them to know because I wasn't sticking around. But with Alex, I opened up as if he were my best friend. It felt natural with him and I couldn't figure out why. I'd be gone in a couple of months and Alex would be nothing but a distant memory like the rest. I set the note down, showered, and got dressed. Since I didn't get the chance to make him breakfast, I decided I was going to make him lunch and bring it to his office.

After preparing Alex's lunch, I hopped in Adam's car and googled the address of Alex's office building. I parked the car in the parking garage and stepped inside the doors of Parker Enterprises. I found the directory on the wall next to a beautiful wall fountain and saw his office was located on the top floor. Of course it was. As I took the elevator up to the thirtieth floor, it suddenly dawned on me that he might be mad I brought him lunch. Oh well, he'd have to get over it. Someone had to make sure he ate properly, and what better person to do it than his chef. The elevator doors opened and his secretary wasn't at her desk and his office door was closed. I lightly knocked and then stepped inside. A wave of shock swept over Alex's face when he looked at me.

"Oh. I'm sorry. Your secretary wasn't at her desk and I didn't know you were in a meeting."

"What are you doing here?" he asked.

The guy sitting in the chair across from his desk turned and looked at me. He looked oddly familiar.

"I brought you lunch." I held up the bag. "I'll just leave it here." I walked inside and set it on the table. "I'm so sorry." I started to sneak out.

"Hey," the guy sitting across from Alex spoke. "I know you." He slowly got up from his chair and walked over to me, checking me out from head to toe.

I looked at Alex, who was shaking his head.

"You must have me mistaken for someone else." I gave a small, fake smile.

"No." He shook his finger at me. "You. That's it! You're that stripper from Vegas."

Alex's eyes widened as he began to walk over to me. I studied the short man with the dark brown hair and the beady eyes.

"You're that man that grabbed my ass and tried to pull me down when I was on stage!"

"Excuse me?" Alex harshly spoke.

"Sorry about that. I had a little too much to drink that night. But I would never forget a hot girly like you and I never forget a face." He smiled. "Are you still stripping?"

"No. I gave that up last year."

Alex's eyes looked like they were about to pop out of his head.

"How do you know Alex here?" he asked.

"I'm his houseguest."

"Lucky man!" The guy patted him on the shoulder. "Anyway, our meeting is over, so the two of you can sit down and eat lunch. "I'll be in touch, Alex."

I watched as Alex took in a sharp inhalation. "We'll talk soon."

As soon as his office door shut, Alex glared at me. "A stripper? Are you kidding me?"

I waved my hand in front of my face. "It was a one-time thing and I didn't get totally naked. I was wearing those nipple covers and I had my thong on. I made a thousand dollars that night." I smirked.

He placed his hand on his head as he continued to glare at me. "Why the hell would you strip in Vegas? Or anywhere, for that matter!"

"A friend of mine was ill that night and if she didn't get someone to replace her, she was going to get fired. She really needed the job because she had a kid to take care of. And I'll have you know that it was a very respectable club. Not one of those trashy ones."

"Jesus, Emerson. I can't even believe you right now."

I frowned. "Does it bother you or something? Hell, I didn't even know you."

"It doesn't matter. You shouldn't have done that. Does Adam know?"

"No, and he won't ever find out. Like I said, it was a one-time thing. Now go and eat your lunch."

"Are you joining me?" he asked calmly.

"Not if you keep having that attitude, I'm not. So I think you need to apologize to me."

"Apologize? For what? For a business client recognizing the girl I fucked as the stripper he groped in Vegas?"

"He said you were a lucky man." I gave a cocky smile.

He rolled his eyes and sighed. "Sit down and have lunch with me," he commanded as he walked over to the table.

I didn't move and stood there with my arms folded.

"SIT!" He pointed to the chair across from him.

****

Alex

As I sat and stared at Emerson from across the table, I couldn't get over the fact that she had stripped in a club full of dirty men who only had one thing on their minds. She could have put her life at risk doing that and I was angry. Why the hell was I angry? I didn't know. All I knew was that it pissed me off.

"Thank you for making me lunch. That was nice of you."

She tilted her head as the corners of her mouth curved up into a beautiful but cocky smile.

"You're welcome. Someone has to look out for your eating habits now that you're on a restricted diet. As long as I'm here, I will be doing just that for you."

"I appreciate it. But I'm not a child. I'm more than capable of watching what I eat."

"All men are children, Alex, and you're no exception." She pointed her finger at me. "I'll train you to eat a proper high blood pressure diet. Then, when I'm gone, you'll be well educated."

Something stirred inside me when she said "when I'm gone." There really was no reason for her to leave so soon after Adam returned. She should use that time to reconnect with her brother.

"Have you thought about sticking around for a while after Adam gets back? Maybe try and reconnect with him?"

"Nah. Never stay in one place too long, and three months back in Cali is way too long."

Her way of thinking was really starting to get on my nerves. After we finished lunch, she left, and I stood looking out the window with my hands in my pockets.

"Excuse me, Mr. Parker?" my secretary Olivia spoke.

"Yes."

"Don't forget you have that charity event tomorrow night at Jonathan Place."

"Shit. I already forgot. Call Jenna and have her make sure my tuxedo is ready."

"Yes, sir."

I sat down at my desk and looked through my contacts of women who would want to attend with me. As I scrolled through the names, no one was peaking my interest. I sighed. Suddenly, I realized that I didn't have Emerson's phone number.

"Olivia," I called over the intercom. "Do some digging and get the phone number for an Emerson James."

"Right away, sir."

"When you get it, text it to my cell."

"Of course, sir."

I'd let her into my home. She cooked for me. I even fucked her twice now and I still didn't have her number. My phone beeped with a text message from Olivia. I stored Emerson's number in my contacts and then sent her a text message.

"There's a charity function tomorrow night and I need you to go with me. You'll need a formal dress, so go to Bloomingdales and buy one. Put it on my account."

A few moments later, she replied, *"Who is this?"*

I rolled my eyes and let a small smile cross my lips.

"It's Alex. Who the hell else would be asking you to a charity event?"

"You never know. Who would have thought I would have run into the man from Vegas in your office, lol!"

Did she really just say "lol"? I shook my head and replied.

"Very funny, Emerson. Now go buy a dress."

"I don't believe you asked me properly, Mr. Parker. You said that you 'need' me to go. You didn't ask me if I would like to go. There's a difference, you know."

I could feel my blood pressure rising by the minute. She was going to be the death of me.

"Emerson, would you like to attend a charity function with me tomorrow night? It's for a very good cause."

"Why thank you, Mr. Parker. I'd love to."

"Good. NOW GO BUY A DRESS!"

"Watch your blood pressure. I would hate to miss that event because you went and had a heart attack."

I clenched my jaw and set my phone down. That woman. That beautiful, hot-as-fuck, amazing-in-bed, smart-mouth woman.

Chapter 16

Emerson

Alex Parker needed to learn some manners on how to ask a woman to an event. How in the world did the women he dated put up with his attitude? I shook my head and walked into the living room where Jenna was dusting and plopped myself on the couch.

"Alex asked me to go to a charity event tomorrow night and he told me to go buy a dress at Bloomingdales."

"Really?" she asked with a twisted face.

"Yeah. I'm just as surprised as you are. Would you like to come with me?"

"When?"

"After you get off work."

"Sure. I'd love to!"

After she was finished with her work for His Majesty, Jenna and I hopped into Adam's car and drove to Bloomingdales. After trying several dresses on, I decided on a beautiful black slim chiffon dress with a sweetheart neckline and beaded top. It was beautiful and it fit perfectly.

"Did Mr. Parker give you a budget?" Jenna asked.

"He just said to put it on his account. But maybe I should ask him. This dress is really expensive."

Pulling out my phone, I sent Alex a text message.

"Hi, it's Emerson. Do I have a budget for the dress?"

"I know who this is, Emerson. Did you find one?"

"Yes."

"How much is it?"

"It's priced at 7,000 dollars."

"Are you kidding me? Is that the only one you could find?"

"Yes. But it's a Christian Dior. I can look around. I saw a pretty dress in the window at a resale shop we passed."

I silently smiled. There would be no way he'd let me buy a dress from a resale shop and be seen with me wearing it.

"Buy the Christian Dior. It's fine."

"Are you sure? I don't mind going to the resale shop."

"EMERSON. BUY THE DAMN DRESS!"

"You don't have to be so rude about it. Remember your blood pressure."

"I'm sorry if I came across rude. Please buy the dress you like. I'm sure you look stunning in it."

"Thank you, Alex."

"You're welcome."

I handed the dress to the sales associate and Jenna and I drove home. When I pulled up, I was surprised to see Alex getting out of the Bentley. It was only eight o'clock. I said goodbye to Jenna and Alex stopped before he reached the front door.

"May I see what you bought?" he asked.

"No. You can see it on me tomorrow night."

We walked into the house and I headed straight to my room, Alex following behind.

"But I paid for it. So I want to see it."

"You will. Tomorrow night." I smiled. "By the way, why are you home so early?"

"I've decided that I'm not going to be at the office so late anymore. I'm going to be doing a lot of work from home."

"Wow. What brought on that revelation?" I smirked.

"I've been working too much and I think it's time I cut back and maybe not worry about so many things."

"So you took my advice?"

"No."

I placed my hand on his muscular chest. "Listen, big guy, we're friends, right?"

"I suppose we're friends. Friends with benefits." The grin on his face grew.

"Right. I guess you could say that. Anyway, I don't know how to break it to you, but you're really uptight and way too proper."

"Excuse me?"

"Don't take offense. You need to let loose a little and stop taking things so seriously. For example, like today in your office, I thought your head was going to explode when you found out about the stripper thing. I did it as a favor. Was I proud? No. But my friend needed me to do it because she's a single mom and she has the most adorable little boy I've ever seen. She really tries to give him a good life and when I heard the manager at the club threaten to fire her, I had to do whatever I could to help. Would I ever do it again? No way. Those men are sex-starved losers who view women as nothing but fuck toys."

"Did you just say fuck toys?"

"Yes. My point is, sometimes you just need to go with the flow. Another example would be how you can't even make yourself a sandwich. You run a multi-billion-dollar company, yet you can't put a piece of meat between two slices of bread."

"Emerson, it's not that I can't make one. I just don't want to. I have people to do that for me."

"My point exactly. What gives you the right to order people around like that?"

"It's how I was raised. We had all kinds of staff in the house that did things for us."

"Of course you did because you're a snob."

The look on his face was getting angrier by the minute.

"I'm not saying this to piss you off. I'm just trying to make you see that you can't control everyone and everything."

"Yes I can," he spoke, deadpan.

I sighed as I rolled my eyes. "I'm going to help you lighten up. It's not like I have anything better to do."

He glared at me, a glare so full of contempt that it was burning a hole through my soul.

"You think you can do that?"

"I know I can." I bit down on my bottom lip.

"Okay, then. Good luck." He turned and walked away.

"You wait and see. By the time I leave California, you'll be a whole new man!" I yelled.

He walked back into the bedroom and cocked his head. "Let me ask you this. Why do you want to change me?"

"I don't want to change you, Alex. I just want you to be more relaxed and appreciate the small things in life and not get so worked up over the little things."

"Are you cooking dinner?" he asked.

"Are you helping?" I smiled.

He took in a deep breath. "Fine. But I don't know how much help I'd actually be."

****

Alex

We stepped into the kitchen and Emerson opened the refrigerator.

"Hmm. Well, it looks like we're making a trip to the grocery store."

"We'll just order take-out," I spoke. There was no way I was going to the grocery store.

"Nope. No takeout for you. Come on, Parker, let's take a trip to the store."

"Can't. Phillip is off for the night."

She raised her eyebrow at me. That right there drove me crazy. I found her incredibly sexy when she did that. She reached inside her purse, grabbed her car keys, and held them up with a smile.

"We don't need Phillip."

"Oh no. We aren't taking Adam's car."

"Yes, we are. It'll be fun. You can drive if you want." She threw me the keys.

I handed her keys back to her. "We'll take my car."

"Your car? Since when do you have a car?" She frowned.

"I've always had a car. Let's go and get this over with." I sighed.

We walked into the grocery store, where Emerson led me to the vegetables.

"See all the pretty colors." She smiled. "Food should be fun and colorful."

At that moment, I caught myself staring at her as she inspected each pepper before putting it into the bag. I found myself smiling on the inside because as much as I hated grocery shopping, I didn't mind it with her.

"Do you like salmon?" she asked as we approached the seafood counter.

"Yes."

"Good, because I make a mean salmon. You're going to love it." She patted my chest.

"I'm sure I will."

Her passion for cooking was undeniable, which led me to think about a few things. As we were on our way home, her phone rang.

"Hey, Adam," she answered and put it on speaker.

"What are you doing?" he asked.

"Alex and I are just heading home from the grocery store."

"What?"

"Did you not hear what I said?"

I let out a light laugh. That attitude of hers.

"Yeah. I heard you. But why?"

"Because I'm cooking dinner for us."

"You better not be sleeping with him, Emerson," he snarled.

She looked over at me and bit down on her lip.

"Okay, so you think because we went to the grocery store that we're sleeping together?"

"Alex doesn't go to the grocery store and the fact that he's with you right now leads me to believe there's something going on."

"Listen, Adam. You sent me to live with him. He hired me to cook for him because his chef had to go to Florida to be with his sick mother. So if you think that grocery shopping with Alex equals sex, then you need therapy. Good-bye, Adam. Call me when you're not going all Freud on me."

She ended the call and I couldn't help but laugh. "He sounded pissed."

"Too bad. I'm tired of him thinking he can run my life. He's not my father and I'm twenty-six years old. Just because he took care of me after the accident doesn't give him the right. By the way, what did my brother do for you that you owed him a favor?"

I looked over at her for a second and then stared back at the road. "He helped me out with the IRS. Let's just say he kept my ass out of jail."

Chapter 17

Emerson

I awoke to the sun peeking through the curtains of the window, my body wrapped comfortably around Alex's. I lay there and watched him sleep for a moment before he opened his eyes and looked at me.

"Good morning."

"Good morning."

"How long have you been awake?" he asked.

"Just a few minutes. I'm going to go cook some breakfast."

As I began to climb out of bed, he reached for my hand. "I'll help."

"Really?" I turned to him with a smile.

"Why not? It wasn't so bad helping you last night with dinner."

"Then let's do it, Parker."

As we climbed out of bed, I slipped into an oversized pink t-shirt and we headed to the kitchen. After grabbing the eggs from the refrigerator, I took out a bowl and asked Alex to crack six eggs.

"Just crack the eggs into this bowl while I cut up the veggies."

"What are we making?" he asked as he poured us each a cup of coffee.

"Vegetable quiche."

As I started to cut up the vegetables, I noticed Alex was having a hard time with the eggs and his finger kept going in the bowl.

"Why are you sticking your finger in the bowl?" I asked.

"Because there's shells in there."

I rolled my eyes and silently laughed. "Don't you know how to crack an egg without getting the shells everywhere?"

"Apparently, I don't." He chuckled.

I set the knife down and took the rest of the eggs, cracking them with one hand and letting them drop into the bowl.

"How the hell did you do that?"

"It's all in the cracking skill, baby." I smiled.

"Did you just call me 'baby'?"

"Yeah. Don't take it too seriously. It's just part of the phrase." I winked.

"Have you ever thought about running your own restaurant?"

"That would mean settling in one place," I spoke as I sliced the onions.

"So. At least you'd be doing what you love."

I didn't want to talk about it anymore. Why was everyone so hell bent on getting me to settle in one place? I changed the subject and finished making the quiche. When it was ready, Alex and I sat down and had breakfast together.

"This is delicious, Emerson. I think I might have to keep you as my personal chef." He winked.

I ignored his comment and asked him to tell me about this charity event we were attending tonight.

"Tell me what this charity event is for."

"It's to help fund an art program for underprivileged kids. Kids who are either homeless, abused, or neglected."

"Good cause." I smiled.

Alex finished his breakfast and got up from the table.

"I'm going into the office for a while. I'll be home later."

"But it's Saturday," I spoke. "What happened to cutting back?"

"I cut back last night and I have a few things I want done before Monday."

"You can't do it at home?"

"No. The files I need are at the office. Are you going to miss me or something?" He smirked.

I frowned. "No. I have my own things to do today. Toodles, Mr. Parker."

"Toodles? Really, Emerson? And what things do you have to do?"

"Just things. Girl things. You wouldn't understand because you're not a girl."

"Okay, then. Go do your girl things and I'll see you later."

He walked out and I cleaned up the breakfast dishes. I couldn't believe he asked me if I was going to miss him. Like, why would I? Just because we had sex didn't mean anything. I had sex with a lot of guys. But it was amazing sex. The best sex I'd ever had in my life. He was a real man in that department. The other men I'd had sex with were boys in men's bodies. They didn't know how to do half the things Alex did and it really sucked that my body craved his touch way too often. It was going to be hard to leave sex with him behind when I left California.

****

Alex

When I arrived at the office, my phone rang. As I pulled it from my pocket, I sighed when I saw Adam's name.

"Hey, Adam. How's Tennessee?"

"Tennessee is fine. I'm going to be blunt here, Alex. Is something going on between you and Emerson?"

"No. Why would you ask that?"

"You're not sleeping with her?"

I cleared my throat. This wasn't a conversation that should be had over the phone.

"No. I'm not."

"She's my sister, man."

"I know that, Adam. What's going on with you?"

"Nothing. I know how you are with women and I don't want my sister to be a part of that."

What the hell was he talking about?

"You know how I am? Do you know how your sister is? How many hearts she's broken all over the world? I nicknamed her 'heartbreaker' until she threatened to break my balls."

He chuckled. "Oh God. Did she really? Sounds like Emerson."

"Yes, she did. I'm going to warn you. Your sister has no plans to stick around."

"Has she talked about where she wants to settle yet?"

"No, and I don't think she's going to settle."

"We'll see about that. Listen, I'm sorry for asking what I did, but I had to make sure."

"I understand. You're her big brother and her protector."

"Yeah. She's all I have left."

"I know."

"How do you know that?"

"She told me about the accident."

"Why? If she told you, then the two of you must be talking a lot."

I sighed.

"I had a health issue and she took me to the hospital. When we were there, she freaked out and had a panic attack. It was after that when she told me."

"Are you okay?"

"I have high blood pressure. Nothing I'm not managing. I'll be fine."

"Sucks, man. I'm sorry to hear that. Is Emerson okay?"

"She's fine."

"Okay. Thanks again for taking her in, even if she's a pain in the ass. I'll talk to you soon, Alex."

"Bye, Adam." *Click.*

I let out a deep breath. If and when he found out I'd been sleeping with his sister, shit was going to hit the fan real hard.

I finished up my work at the office and headed home to shower and get ready for the charity event. As I walked through the door, I looked around for Emerson. I knew she was home because Adam's car was in the driveway. I went to her room and knocked on the door.

"Emerson, are you in there?"

"Yes, but you can't come in. I'm getting ready."

"Okay. I'm going upstairs to shower and get dressed. I'll meet you in the foyer in an hour."

"I'll be ready," she yelled.

Once I was dressed, I walked down the stairs and stopped midway when I saw Emerson standing in the foyer. When she turned and looked at me, she took my breath away. She looked so stunning that I was speechless.

"What's wrong with you?" She smiled with her red lips.

"Nothing. You look beautiful." I made my way down the stairs.

"Thank you, Parker. You look very handsome in that tuxedo." She reached for my bowtie.

The black Christian Dior dress she wore was captivating, as was the way she wore her hair pinned up with a few strands of curls hanging down. Her face was painted with makeup to perfection and she was by far the most beautiful and elegant woman that I'd ever laid eyes on.

Chapter 18

Emerson

We climbed in the back of the Bentley and headed to the charity event. Alex reached over and took hold of my hand.

"There's something I need to tell you, but I don't want you to get mad."

"You sound serious."

"Adam called me today and demanded to know if we are sleeping together."

I rolled my eyes and sighed. "What did you tell him?"

"I told him no."

"Did he believe you?"

"I think so. He can't find out what we did."

"It's none of his damn business. But don't worry, I'm not telling him anything. Why are you so afraid of him?"

"I'm not. It's a friend code sort of thing."

"Ah, I see." I smirked. "Some friend he is that he couldn't even tell you about his family or even mention that he had a sister who was alive."

The fact that my brother was so concerned about who I was sleeping with irked me. I shrugged it off. He was going to be a lot to deal with when he came back. We climbed out of the Bentley and Alex held out his arm to me.

****

As I stepped inside the ballroom of the Four Seasons Hotel, I was enthralled by the beauty of it. The light-filled space was decorated beautifully with silver tablecloths that covered each table with illuminated floral centerpieces that easily became the focal point of the entire room.

"There are very influential people here tonight, so can I trust that you'll be on your best behavior?"

"I'm always on my best behavior." I frowned.

"As long as you don't open your mouth, we should be good."

I lightly took my heel and discreetly kicked him.

"Ouch. What was that for?"

"Your rudeness." I put on a fake smile as a distinguished-looking man walked towards us.

"Good to see you, Alex." He smiled as they shook hands.

"Good to see you, Edward."

Edward looked me up and down before taking hold of my hand and bringing it up to his lips.

"And who, may I ask, is this beautiful woman on your arm?"

"Edward this is my friend, Emerson James. Emerson, please meet Edward Hollings."

"It's nice to meet you, Edward."

"Believe me when I say the pleasure is all mine, Emerson. You are a very stunning woman."

"Thank you." I smiled.

After their light conversation, Alex and I went to the bar for a drink.

"Glass of wine?" he asked.

"Yes, please. Pinot would be great."

He turned his back and flagged down the bartender. As I looked around the room, I heard a voice behind me.

"Emerson, is that you?" The familiar voice made a pit in my stomach.

I slowly turned around and gulped.

"Christian?"

"Oh my God, it is you." He smiled. "I didn't know you were back in California. What's it been? Eight years?"

"Yes, and I'm only here temporarily. I'll be leaving soon."

"You look amazing."

I heard Alex clear his throat as he handed me my Pinot.

"Alex Parker, this is Christian Billings. Christian, meet Alex Parker."

The two of them shook hands and I could sense something off with Alex.

"So how do the two of you know each other?" he asked.

I graciously smiled at Christian. "Would you like to tell him or should I?"

"We used to date when we were teenagers," he spoke nervously as he looked at me.

I placed my hand on his chest. "Oh come on, Chris."

"Oh boy," I heard Alex mumble.

"Chris and I had been dating for almost a year before the accident. When I woke up from the coma, I was told by my friends that he broke up with me and went off to college." I laughed.

"Emerson, I—"

"Save it, Billings. You're a total douchebag for doing that. At least you could have had the common courtesy to wait until I woke up. You never called me to explain why you left and you never checked to see how I was doing. Not only did I lose my twin sister and parents, but I also lost the one person who I thought would always be there for me. And you know why?" I tilted my head. "Because you said you loved me."

"I'm sorry. I didn't know if you'd ever wake up and I couldn't put my life on hold waiting for you. Now if you'll excuse me, I am going to walk away from this conversation."

"No. Please, Christian, let me do the walking this time." I lightly placed my hand on his arm as I took my Pinot and walked away. Alex followed behind.

"I'm sorry."

I rolled my eyes. "Don't be. Best thing that ever happened to me."

"You never mentioned him when you were telling me about the accident."

"He wasn't worth mentioning."

Alex mixed and mingled with the elite while I stayed in the background and watched as people pulled out their checkbooks. I left his side to go to the bar for another glass of Pinot. He was so busy chatting that he didn't even notice I had left. Sipping on my wine from the barstool and looking around, I noticed Alex was gone. I got up and walked around the ballroom, but I didn't see him. As I stepped out into the lobby of the hotel, I saw him kissing a tall, elegant-looking woman with curly but frizzy brown hair. My heart started to pick up the pace as my stomach bottomed out. I quickly turned around and walked out of the Four Seasons Hotel. I wasn't exactly sure what I was feeling at that moment, but I couldn't let on what I saw. My phone dinged with a text message from Alex.

"Where are you?"

I took in a deep breath before responding.

"Outside. I just needed some fresh air."

A few moments later, Alex walked up behind me.

"Are you feeling okay?"

"Yeah. It was just a little stuffy in there." I gave a small smile.

"Are you referring to the air or the people?" He grinned.

"Maybe both."

"Well, dinner is about to be served. So let's go inside and have a nice meal and we'll leave after."

"Okay."

The last thing I wanted to do was go back inside and see the woman he was kissing. Alex led us over to our table and he was gracious enough to pull out my chair for me.

"Thanks."

He gave me a nod and took his seat next to me. As dinner was being served, I looked at the table next to us and there she was, staring at me. Or should I say, glaring at me. As I placed my napkin on my lap, I glanced over at Alex.

"That woman over there keeps staring at me."

He looked at her and she quickly turned away. "Maybe she's jealous of you."

"Why would she be jealous of me?"

"I don't know, Emerson." His tone sounded irritated.

I ate dinner in silence while Alex talked amongst the others around the table.

Chapter 19

Alex

I hadn't seen Bella in almost five years. Seeing her tonight was a total shock at best. It wasn't something I had planned on. Hell, I didn't even know she was back in L.A. Emerson was being quiet and it bothered me. She was never this quiet and I got the impression something was wrong. When I found her outside, she said she was fine, but I didn't believe her. I bet it was seeing her ex-boyfriend. I made a promise to myself five years ago to never let another woman get to me. I'd made good on that promise because I never dated anyone too long to let things get serious. Much like Emerson, once they started showing signs of wanting a commitment of some sort, it was time to leave; to walk away and find the next person with the hopes they just wanted to have a casual fling. That was what Emerson wanted. Her thinking was very much like mine and I was grateful for that. Tonight, we had something in common. We both saw our exes after a number of years and old wounds were reopened.

I looked over at Emerson, who was on her third glass of wine. She kept staring over at Bella and it made me uncomfortable.

"I see you staring at that woman over there. Why do you keep doing that?" I asked.

"Why not? She was staring at me first. I think she's very pretty except for that mess of curly hair. She really should see a stylist about those ends."

I chuckled as I took the glass of wine from her hand. "I think you've had enough wine."

Her head tilted as she took the glass back from me. "Who are you? The wine keeper?" She brought the glass up to her lips and finished it off in one swallow.

"I'm afraid I'm going to have to cut you off now," I spoke with authority.

She put her hand to my face. "You can't and won't tell me when I've had enough."

"Emerson, I'm warning you." I looked around at the table to make sure nobody heard her.

She grabbed my cheek and pinched it. "You're so fucking cute when you think you're in control."

"Okay. Let's go. We need to get you home." I softly took hold of her arm.

She let out a light laugh. "I don't have a home, Parker. I'm homeless."

I put my arm around her to make sure she didn't fall over. As we were walking out of the ballroom, Bella was standing in the lobby with some guy.

"That man she's with is sexy." Emerson smiled as she looked at me.

"No he's not."

"Jealous?"

"Why the hell would I be jealous?"

She didn't answer me. When we stepped outside the hotel, Phillip was there, holding the car door open. I helped Emerson in the back seat and climbed in next to her.

"I think I need to lie down."

"Lay your head on my lap."

"You're not going to get a boner, are you?" She smirked.

"Emerson, just lay your damn head down and close your eyes," I spoke in irritation but on the inside, I was smiling.

When we arrived home, I helped her out of the Bentley and then picked her up, carrying her into the house and to her room as she laid her head on my chest. I set her down and unzipped her dress, letting it fall to the ground. Her body was a dream and I wanted nothing more than to fuck her into oblivion. But I wouldn't. She had too much to drink and I would never take advantage. I grabbed the nightshirt that she had sitting on the bed and slipped it over her head. Pulling back the covers, I helped her climb in, and the moment her head hit the pillow, her eyes closed. Softly kissing her forehead, I placed the back of my hand on her cheek.

"Sleep well, Emerson James."

****

Emerson

As I lay in bed, I couldn't help thinking about what I had seen last night between Alex and frizzy curly-haired girl. Seeing them kissing cut deep into my soul and it pissed me off.

Why? I couldn't tell you. I liked Alex a lot and he was there with me, not her. For him to go off and kiss another woman when he was with a woman was a total douchebag move. And then to sit at the table and pretend not to know her was even worse. I gave him the opportunity to tell me, but he didn't. He played dumb. Typical man. I was going to put an end to my wandering thoughts so I climbed out of bed and marched to the kitchen. He wasn't there. I stomped up the stairs and opened his bedroom door. He wasn't there. I walked through the entire house and I couldn't find him. It was apparent he wasn't home. Where the hell did he go? It was Sunday.

As I stood and watched the coffee brew, mug gripped tightly in my hand, waiting for it to finish, the patio door opened and Alex walked in. He was drenched in sweat.

"Good morning," he spoke as he wiped his face with a towel.

"Where were you?" I demanded to know.

"I went for a run. Can't you tell?" He smirked. "I'm surprised you're up already. I figured you'd be in bed all day, hung over."

"Is there a reason why you didn't make coffee when you woke up?" I asked with an attitude.

"I wanted to wait until I got back. I don't like to run after drinking coffee."

It was gnawing at me. The question that I had since last night. "Are you going to tell me who the frizzy curly-haired woman was that you were kissing last night?"

His eyes narrowed at me and he pursed his lips. Leaning against the counter, he folded his arms.

"No. Actually, I'm not going to tell you. I'm sorry you saw that."

"Sorry? You're sorry? Fuck, Alex. Could you be any more of a douchebag?"

"A what?" He cocked his head.

I took my phone from the counter, googled the word "douchebag," and handed it to him.

He arched his brow as he read it out loud from the Urban Dictionary site. "'Someone who has surpassed the levels of jerk and asshole; however, not yet reached fucker or motherfucker.' Well, at least I'm not a fucker."

"Not yet anyway, but you're sure close."

"Umm. You just received a text message from someone named Keith."

I grabbed my phone from his hand and looked at it. Rolling my eyes, I set my phone down and poured myself a cup of coffee.

"Are you going to tell me who Keith is?"

"Actually, I'm not going to tell you. I'm sorry you saw that." I took my phone and my coffee and strutted to my room, shutting the door behind me.

****

Alex

I watched as she walked her sexy ass, which was barely covered by her shirt, away from me. And who the hell was Keith? Why did a fire erupt inside me when I saw his name? It was none of my business, just like Bella was none of hers. As I left the kitchen and started walking up the stairs, I heard Emerson's voice.

"You can't shut me out, Parker. We're friends and friends talk. I told you things that I had never told anyone before."

Standing on the steps, I turned and looked at her. "You expect me to believe that in all your worldly travels and of all the men you've fucked, you never spoke about your family or the accident?"

"Yes, I do expect you to believe it because it's true. I'd never opened up like that to anyone."

Narrowing my eyes, I slowly walked down the stairs until I was standing in front of her.

"Why me, Emerson?"

"I don't really know, Alex. Maybe because it's being back here and you were there."

I placed my hand on her cheek and stared into her beautiful eyes.

"I appreciate you telling me, but I'm not talking to you about Bella. There are some things that are off limits."

"Oh really?" She backed away. "Guess what? There are some things that are off limits for me as well and that includes sex. Bye, Felicia," she spoke as she put up her hand and walked away.

"What? Who the fuck is Felicia?" I yelled.

I placed my hands on my head and went upstairs. Slamming the door, I took a shower to cool off. I could feel my blood pressure rising because of one Miss Emerson James and I was no longer going to stand for it.

Chapter 20

Emerson

"There are some things that are off limits, my ass," I mumbled as I showered and got dressed. He was irritating the fuck out of me and the best thing to do was separate myself from him for a while. I was suffocating here anyway. I packed a small bag and climbed into Adam's car. I was taking a road trip to Napa Valley, the one place that me and my sister always said that when we were of drinking age, we'd go visit and get drunk off the amazing wine they had there. I never had the chance to go because I left California when I was eighteen. But now that I was back for a short period of time and Alex Parker was being nothing but a douchebag, I was off to explore the wineries. I had one credit card that I saved for emergency purposes only and this was an emergency situation. As I was making my seven-hour drive to Napa, my phone rang. It was Adam.

"Hello."

"Hi, Em. I was just calling to see how you're doing."

"I'm good. I hope you don't mind, but I'm taking your car to Napa Valley."

"WHAT?! Why the hell are you going to Napa Valley?"

"I needed to get out of that house. I was suffocating, and me and Emily always wanted to go there. Adam, tomorrow is the anniversary of their death. This is something I need to do."

"I know what tomorrow is, Em, and I wish I could be back in California with you. But I can't."

"I know you can't and it doesn't matter anyway. I've spent the last eight anniversaries alone, so tomorrow will be no different."

"Emerson, I'm—"

"No need to say it, big brother. I already know."

"Do you need some money?" he asked.

"No. I have cash and a credit card that I have saved for emergencies."

"Okay. Have a safe trip, and if you need anything, call me."

"Thanks. I will." *Click.*

As I was driving down the highway, I pulled up the playlist on my phone and played "Don't Look Back in Anger" by Oasis. It was our favorite song in the whole world and we sang it together almost every day. I turned up the volume and rolled all the windows down. I began to sing it as loudly as I could as the warm breeze swept over my face.

As I pulled up to the Wine Country Inn bed and breakfast, I prayed they had a room available. If not, then I would have to find somewhere else in Napa. When I walked into the lobby, a blond-haired woman smiled at me from behind the desk.

"Hello. Welcome to Wine Country Inn. How can I help you?"

"I'm hoping you have a room available. This was a last-minute trip and I didn't call to make a reservation."

"Ah. How many guests?" she asked.

"Just me." I smiled.

She looked at me as she checked her computer. "We have one room available and it's our Private Vineyard View King Cottage for $615.00 a night."

"Ouch. That's the only room you have?"

"Yes. How long are you planning on staying?"

"I don't know. A few days maybe."

"On Tuesday, we have one of our standard rooms available. If you want, you can stay in the cottage for two nights and then we can switch you over to one of the other cheaper rooms."

I twisted my face, unsure of what to do. Six hundred fifteen dollars a night was more than I was planning on spending. But, if it was only for two nights, I could manage it and it was surely beautiful here.

"Fine. I'll take it." I smiled.

"Excellent. I'll just need your driver's license and credit card."

Once she input my information, she handed me the keys to the cottage and gave me directions as to its location. Upon opening the door, I stepped inside and the first word out of my mouth was "Wow." I could see why this place was expensive. The room featured a small living area with a loveseat and a chair that sat across from a fireplace with a TV mounted above it. Behind the living area were three steps that led up to the king-sized bed with a large window that faced the vineyards. Setting my bag on the bed, I began to unpack and put my clothes away in the three-drawer dresser that sat against the wall. When I heard my phone ding from my purse, I grabbed it and found a text message from Alex.

"Where the hell are you? You've been gone all day. It's nighttime and I would like to know that you're safe."

Did I answer him? Where I was, was none of his concern. He wasn't my keeper. But I didn't want him to worry and get his blood pressure all high, so I replied.

"I'm safe and I'm fine. I took a little road trip and I'll be gone probably at least four days. Make sure to take your blood pressure medication and lay off the salt."

"A road trip? TO WHERE?"

"I appreciate you asking, but I'm not talking to you about where I am. It's somewhere I needed to be."

"EMERSON JAMES! WHERE DID YOU GO?!"

"Calm yourself, Parker. I'm fine. Are you going to miss me or something? You should be happy I'm gone. Now I can't bug you about frizzy curly-haired girl."

I silently laughed to myself.

"Emerson, please tell me where you are."

"That's a no for me, Parker. Enjoy your week and I'll see you when I get back."

****

Alex

I stood there, staring at her message in anger. "That's a no for me." Was she serious? She and that mouth of hers was killing me. Who the hell did she think she was? A small smile crossed my lips. She was Emerson James, a fierce, not-to-be-fucked-with type of girl who did whatever the hell she wanted to. No boundaries, no rules, and not a care in the world. I didn't know her when she was off gallivanting around the world, so I couldn't care. But now I knew her and I cared about her and her safety. Fuck, I cared way more than that. She had gotten under my skin and somehow into my heart. I dialed Adam to tell him his sister had left.

"Hey, Alex. What's up, man?"

"Your mouthy and defiant sister took off and went somewhere for a few days."

"Yeah. I know. I talked to her earlier."

"Where did she go? She won't tell me."

I heard him chuckle. "Did you two have a fight or something?"

"No. Yes. Well, sort of."

"Jesus. What is going on with the two of you?"

"Nothing. We're friends and I'm concerned for her safety."

"You don't need to worry about Emerson, Alex. She's been doing this for eight years."

"It doesn't matter. She's a young woman all alone in a strange place."

"What are you going to do? Go to where she is?"

"Maybe."

"Oh my God, Alex. You've fallen for her. Haven't you?"

"I don't want to discuss it over the phone."

"Well, you have no choice, bro, because I can't be in California. So you better fucking tell me what's going on between you and my sister."

I silenced myself for a moment. If I wanted to know where she was, I'd have to tell him.

"I may have developed some feelings for her."

"Jesus Christ. You're serious. Aren't you?"

"Yes."

"I'll ask you one last time. Did you sleep with her?"

"Yes."

Silence crowded the other end of the phone.

"The two of you had a fight? You haven't known each other long enough to fight yet."

"I know, but she's Emerson."

"True and you're Alex Parker. The two of you couldn't be more opposite. God, Alex. Why?"

"We can't help who we fall for. It's just there, Adam."

"Fine." He sighed. "She's in Napa Valley. Fuck, I can't believe I'm telling you this. It's a place she and Emily always wanted to visit. Tomorrow is the anniversary of her and my parents' death. Emerson has spent too many years alone on that day and I don't want her alone again. Promise me you'll go to Napa and be with her as a friend, Alex."

"I will. Where is she staying?"

"I don't know. She didn't say, but I'll do some checking and see if I can find out through her credit card. I'll call you back." *Click.*

So she went to Napa Valley. I loved Napa Valley, and it wasn't a place that should be seen alone. I took my suitcase from my closet and began packing some clothes. A few moments later, my phone rang and it was Adam.

"Did you find out?"

"Yeah. She's at the Wine Country Inn. I'll send you the address. Don't tell her that I told you."

"I won't. I promise. Thanks, Adam. I appreciate it."

"You owe me again, Alex. I know my sister, so don't come crying to me when she breaks your heart."

"I'll remember that. I'll talk to you soon."

I ended the call and immediately called my pilot, Warren.

"Hello, Mr. Parker."

"Warren, I need you to fuel up the plane for tomorrow morning and take me to Napa Valley. We'll leave around nine o'clock."

"It'll be ready, sir."

"Thank you." *Click.*

I sighed as I tossed my phone on the bed. Was I doing the right thing? Hell if I knew. The only thing I did know was that she shouldn't be spending tomorrow alone.

****

When we landed at the Napa County Airport, I had a car waiting for me to take me to the Wine Country Inn. When I walked into the lobby, a blonde-haired woman smiled at me from behind the desk.

"Welcome to the Wine Country Inn. How can I help you?"

"I'm looking for one of your guests. She checked in yesterday and her name is Emerson James."

"I'm sorry, sir, but I cannot give out that type of information."

"Please." I glanced at her name badge. "Noelle. It's very important."

"Again, sir. We are not allowed to give out our guests' information."

I reached into my pocket and pulled out a hundred-dollar bill. "See this. It's all yours if you tell which room she is staying in."

"You're going to have to leave before I call the police."

I sighed. "Listen, please. She's a close friend of mine and today is the anniversary of her twin sister's and parents' death. I don't want her to be alone. I'll give you my credit card information and my driver's license. Anything you need. I'm not a murderer or a rapist. I'm her friend and I'm here to make sure she gets through this day."

"Then I'll call her room and let her know you're here."

"No. It's a surprise." I smiled. I reached in my pocket and pulled out my wallet. "Here is my credit card. I want you to use this to pay for her stay here."

She glared at me and then took the card from my hand. "I'll also need your driver's license."

"Here you go." I handed it to her.

She typed on her computer and handed me back my credit card and license.

"She's in cottage five. Go out the door, make a right, go down the trail a bit, and you'll see a line of cottages. She's the last one on the right."

"Thank you, Noelle." I smiled as I handed her the hundred-dollar bill.

"You're welcome, Mr. Parker."

Chapter 21

Emerson

I awoke to the morning sun beaming through the window. Rolling over, I stared at the beauty of the vineyards that graced the area.

"Hi, Emily. Mom and Dad. I'm doing okay. I'm here in Napa, sis. Just like we always talked about. It's so beautiful here. Well, from what I can see out the window. I just got in last night and I haven't had a chance to explore yet, but I will as soon as I get some coffee and get dressed. Give me a sign that you're here with me."

Climbing out of bed, I showered, got dressed, and popped a k-cup in the Keurig they so graciously provided in the room. As the coffee filled the cup, there was a knock on the door.

"Room service."

I frowned. They must have the wrong room. Opening the door, I froze when I saw Alex standing there with a cart.

"Alex, what the—"

"Good morning, Emerson." The corners of his mouth curved into a smile.

"What are you doing here?"

"I brought you breakfast. I hope you haven't eaten already."

"You came all the way from Malibu to bring me breakfast?"

"Something like that." He winked. "Are you going to let me in or are we going to stand here and debate while our breakfast gets cold."

I waved my hand and stepped aside, letting him inside the cottage. I couldn't help but let out a light laugh as I watched him wheel the cart in.

"What's so funny?"

"You. Wheeling that cart in like you're the help. How did you know where I was?"

"I have my ways, Emerson. Since you refused to tell me last night, I had no choice but to do some digging on my own. Now come and eat."

"What if I don't want you here?" I asked as I narrowed my eyes at him.

"You do." He smirked.

"No, actually, I don't. Do you not remember our conversation yesterday?"

"Yes. I remember it well. Now sit down and eat."

I walked over to the table where he had set the plates of food. He removed the metal cover, revealing a plate of eggs, bacon, fresh fruit, and toast. He picked up the carafe and poured coffee into the white ceramic mug.

"Thank you," I spoke as I sat down.

"You're welcome."

Placing the napkin on my lap, I looked at Alex.

"You shouldn't have come."

"Why not?"

"Did it ever occur to you that I left to get away from you?"

He shrugged. "Yes, and I away from you. But the truth is you're glad I'm here," he smugly spoke. He looked around the cottage. "This is very nice. I approve."

"It's all they had available."

"Nice bed. Is it comfortable?"

"Very comfortable. I slept like a baby last night."

He took a bite of his eggs. "Good. Then I'm happy to know that I'll be sleeping like a baby tonight."

My eyes darted up at him as I grabbed my coffee. "Excuse me? You aren't sleeping in that bed. If you're planning on staying, you better get your own room."

"Can't. They don't have anything available and since I'm paying for this room, I'll be sleeping in that bed right there."

I laughed. "I'm paying for this room. This is my room."

"Correction, Emerson. I'm paying for this room. I gave Noelle my credit card and told her to charge the entire stay on it."

"Who the fuck is Noelle?"

"Who the fuck is Felicia?" He grinned.

"You really do live in your own little uptight world. Don't you?"

"Yes. I suppose I do. Noelle is the blonde at the front desk."

"Ah. I see. So she told you what cottage I was in. Isn't that against policy or something? What if you were here to murder me?"

"Money talks, baby. I slipped her a hundred for the info."

"Did you just call me 'baby'?" I narrowed my eyes at him.

"Yeah. Don't take it too seriously. It's just part of the phrase." He winked and, suddenly, my panties melted.

"You can't steal my lines." I pointed my fork at him.

He chuckled. "So what are we doing today?"

"I'm going to explore Napa. I don't know what you're doing."

"Guess I'm exploring Napa with you."

I sighed and then looked down. Placing my napkin on the table, I got up from my seat.

"Today's not really a good day, Alex, and I prefer to spend it alone."

He got up from his chair and walked over to me. "I know what today is."

"How?"

He didn't answer me. His eyes just stared into mine and I knew at that moment how he knew where I was.

"Oh my God! Adam told you. Didn't he? He told you I was here."

"I promised I wouldn't say. But he didn't want you to be alone."

"He didn't want? What about what I want? Damn him!"

Alex clasped my shoulders. "If you really want me to go, I will."

His scent. That damn scent got me every time. Fuck my pheromones.

"You came all the way here, so you might as well stay. By the way, how did you get here?"

The corners of his mouth curved up. "There's these things and they're called planes. Maybe you heard of them."

I smacked his chest and smiled as he pulled me into him.

"Emerson, I'm sorry about yesterday."

"You suck, Parker. But apology accepted." I smiled up at him.

"Are you going to tell me who Felicia is?"

"Are you still on that?" I reached for my phone and googled "Bye, Felicia" and handed it to him.

His eyebrow arched as he read the definition out loud from the Urban Dictionary site. "When someone says that they're leaving and you could really give two shits less that they are. Their name then becomes 'Felicia,' a random bitch that nobody is sad to see go. Their real name becomes irrelevant because nobody cares what it really is. Instead, they now are 'Felicia.' I think I'm insulted."

"You should be." I grinned.

He leaned in, his lips mere inches from mine, his scent soaking my panties. "I think I need to kiss that sassy mouth of yours."

"Oh yeah? What if I don't want you to," I whispered.

"You do." His lips softly brushed against mine.

Our soft kiss became passionate as our tongues met once again. The ache down below was fierce and I was on fire with desire to feel him inside of me. Suddenly, I heard something. I broke our kiss and stared at him.

"Do you hear that?" A smile beamed across my face.

"Hear what?"

"Come on!" I grabbed his hand and flew out the door.

"Emerson, stop. We're going to get wet."

"Alex, it's raining. The rain was my and Emily's thing. We loved it," I spoke as we stood on the cobbled walkway in front of the gardens while the rain fell down on us. I began to turn in a circle, holding my hands up to the sky with a smile across my face. "This is because of Emily. I asked her earlier to give me a sign that she was here. This is her sign." I smiled as I looked at Alex.

"Of course she's here with you." He took hold of my hand.

The smile never left my face as I looked up at the sky, letting the rain hit my face.

"Come on." I pulled him behind me.

"Where are we going?"

"For a walk in the rain. Sometimes, Emily and I would walk until it stopped. We always said that the rain washed away the sins of the past. It cleansed our souls, so to speak."

"Do you think that maybe we can grab an umbrella?"

I looked at him and shook my head. "No, Alex. Don't you see the beauty of the rain?"

"Umm. I don't see what the beauty is in getting soaking wet."

I sighed.

"You take a shower, right?"

"Of course."

"Why do you take showers?"

He stared at me blankly. "To get clean."

"Exactly! The rain is pure. A gift from God. It cleanses the land, helps things grow." I let go of his hand and started walking backwards so I was facing him. "You take a shower or bath to cleanse your body, but you walk in the rain to cleanse your heart and soul."

"Oh," he spoke.

I laughed. "Feel the rain. Lift your hands up and feel the way it falls on your hands." I took his hands and faced them upwards. A small smile fell upon his lips as he stared at me.

"I'm sure your soul needs a lot of cleansing. Take it all in, Parker."

"Thanks, Emerson." He frowned.

I laughed as I let go of his hands and picked up the pace in front of him. Before I knew it, he came up from behind and wrapped his arms tightly around my waist. I stopped, placing my hands on his arms.

"What are you doing?"

"Taking in all the beauty." He kissed my cheek.

Chapter 22

Alex

Watching her dance in the rain was one of the most beautiful things I'd ever seen. The way she viewed life and things were so different from the way I viewed them, but yet, the way she did started making sense to me.

I let go of her and she turned around and looked at me, wiping the rain from my face.

"We can go back to the cottage if you want."

I gave her a small smile as I placed my hands on each side of her face. "No. Let's walk a while longer."

The corners of her mouth curved upwards and I hooked my arm around her as we continued our journey in the rain. Suddenly, out of nowhere, the rain stopped and the sun reappeared.

"Guess it's time to go back now and change out of these wet clothes." She smiled.

"Let's go."

When we entered the cottage, the first thing I did was kick off my shoes and take off my wet shirt before starting the water for a bath.

"What are you doing? Are you taking a shower?" she asked as she began to strip out of her wet clothes.

"*We* are taking a bath together."

"Oh?" She arched her brow.

I took off my soaking wet pants and boxers and held my hand out to her. "Are you coming?"

"You tell me." She bit down on her sexy lip.

"Get over here."

She walked towards me and took my hand. As I led her into the bathroom, she stopped me as I was about to climb into the bathtub.

"Stop."

"What's wrong?" I asked.

"There's no bubbles."

"Really? Do we really need bubbles?"

"Yes, we do, Parker. It's customary when you take a bath with someone, you do it in a bubble-filled tub."

She reached for the bottle that was labeled "Lavender bubble bath" from the shelf and poured more than a capful into the water.

I sighed. "Now I'm going to smell like a girl."

She patted my cheek. "Shut up and get in the tub."

I chuckled as I climbed in the oversized tub with my back against it. With the help of my hand, Emerson climbed in and nestled her back tightly against my chest as my arms wrapped securely around her. We sat there in silence for a moment and I pressed my lips against her head and she ran her fingers up and down my arm.

"We had dated for over a year."

Her eyes darted up to mine. "Huh? Who?"

"Bella and I. Or, as you call her, 'frizzy curly-haired woman.'"

"Oops. Sorry about that."

"Things were great with us, or at least I thought they were. We talked about a future together. Our jobs, buying a house, settling in."

"What happened?"

"One day while we were having lunch, she got a call and a job offer from an advertising agency in New York. Hell, I didn't even know she had applied for it."

"She didn't tell you?"

"Nope. She told me she was going to New York to visit her best friend."

"Wow. She sucks."

"We got into a huge fight about it when she told me she was accepting their offer. She told me that I was a very selfish man and that I couldn't stand to see her make something of herself and that I never supported her decisions."

"Was that true?"

"No. It was the fact that she didn't tell me about it in the first place. She had lied to me and that's something I don't tolerate."

"Why did she feel like she had to lie to you?"

"I asked that very question and she couldn't answer me. Finally, after hours of arguing, she said that she wasn't happy and she was leaving."

"Just like that?" she asked as she looked up at me.

"Yep. Just like that. The next day, she was gone without so much as a goodbye."

"I'm sorry, Alex. That must have been hard on you."

"It was for a while."

"Were you in love with her?"

"I thought I was, even though I never told her, but her leaving made me realize that I wasn't. She used to tell me that she loved me and the only response I would give was "me too."

She narrowed her eyes at me and, with a tilted head, she spoke, "That's what I would always say. The only guy I ever said those three words to was asshole Christian. But it didn't count because I was sixteen and sixteen-year-olds just spew out those words as if it means nothing. Actually, it doesn't mean anything at that age because sixteen-year-olds don't even know what love is."

"But you thought you loved him." I smiled.

"Thinking it and actually being in it are two different things. I can actually sit here and tell you that I have no idea what real love between a guy and a girl is."

"Let's look it up." I smiled as I reached over from the tub and grabbed my phone from the small table that sat next to it. After I Googled the word "love," I pulled the definition from the Urban Dictionary since she seemed so fond of that site. I held it up in front of her to read out loud.

Before reading it, she looked up at me. "Wow. That's an awful long definition, but here I go. Love is the most spectacular, indescribable, deep, euphoric feeling for someone. Love is an incredibly powerful word. When you're in love, you always want to be together, and when you're not, you're thinking about being together because you need that person and, without them, your life is incomplete. This love is unconditional affection with no limits or conditions: completely loving someone. It's when you trust the other with your life and when you would do anything for each other. When you love someone, you want nothing more than for them to be truly happy no matter what it takes because that's how much you care about them and because their needs come before your own. You hide nothing of yourself and can tell the other anything because you know they accept you just the way you are and vice versa. It's when they're the last thing you think about before you go to sleep, and when they're the first thing you think of when you wake up, the feeling that warms your heart and leaves you overcome by a feeling of serenity. Love involves wanting to show your affection and/or devotion to each other. It's the smile on your face you get when you're thinking about them and miss them. Love can make you do anything and sacrifice for what will be better in the end. Love is intense and passionate. Everything seems brighter, happier, and more wonderful when you're in love. If you find it, don't let it go."

"Nicely done," I spoke as I set down my phone. "I can officially say that I have never been in love." I chuckled.

She let out a light laugh. “Me neither. So why were you kissing her?”

“I wasn’t kissing her. You must have seen us when she kissed me. The minute her lips hit mine, I pushed her away. She told me that she regretted leaving me and she was hoping that maybe we could try again.”

“How long ago did the two of you break up?”

“Five years ago. It was right before my father passed away. After she left and I thought about all the time wasted with her, I made a vow never to attach myself to one person again.”

“I understand. So you went on a heart-breaking spree instead.”

“Look who’s talking.” I chuckled.

“I know. I guess we have more in common than we thought we did.” She smiled.

“It seems that way. Doesn’t it?”

“So after five years, she just thought you’d take her back?”

“I guess.”

“Must be that frizzy, curly hair.” She laughed.

I laughed with her as my grip around her tightened. “So now you know about Bella. Now who is Keith?”

She sighed. “A dogsled racer from Alaska.”

“What? You went to Alaska? Why?”

“Because Emily and I really wanted to see for ourselves if it stayed dark all day for long periods of time.”

"Well, that depends on where you are in Alaska. Doesn't it?"

"Yes, and where I was, it stayed dark or dusk all day during the winter months. But it was beautiful there."

"Why did you leave?"

"Never stay in one place too long, Parker. Plus, after two months of no sunlight, I couldn't take it anymore."

"And Keith?"

"Keith was a nice guy. I never slept with him or anything. We went out a few times and had some fun. Occasionally, he will call or text me just to find out how I'm doing."

My hands roamed to her breasts and began massaging them lightly. I had held off long enough without touching her and my cock was ready to devour her. She closed her eyes and let out a low moan as my fingers played with her hardened nipples. My tongue explored her neck as she tilted her head to the side. My cock was semi-hard when she nestled against me, but now it was rapidly rising in excitement. She turned around and wrapped her legs around me as I slowly entered her. Her hands planted firmly on my shoulders as we stared into each other's eyes while she slowly moved up and down. Our lips met with seduction and her pace was slow and steady. Moans escaped us in between kisses as the pressure was building. I reached my hand under the water and pressed my finger against her clit, heightening her pleasure as she circled her hips around my cock. She threw her head back as my tongue slid down her throat while she reached the peak of her orgasm, causing me to lose control and spill everything I had deep inside her. Our eyes locked and it was at that moment that I knew I was falling deep and hard for her and it scared the living fuck out of me.

Chapter 23

Emerson

After a long day and a lot wine, Alex and I settled into bed. I took my phone from the nightstand and brought up the video of me and Emily in the car, singing "Don't Look Back in Anger." I handed my phone to him to watch.

"I've always liked this song." He smiled.

"It was our favorite song."

"When was this taken?"

"The day of the accident." A tear formed in my eye. "About an hour before."

"She looks exactly like you. If she were here, I honestly don't know if I could tell you apart."

"She had a birthmark on her right hip. That was how my parents could tell us apart when we were babies."

"Did you ever pull the twin switch on a guy?"

I laughed. "Once. Right before our sixteenth birthday, Emily was dating this guy, and he was really needy and clingy. She didn't want to see him anymore but didn't have the heart to break his heart. So, I did it for her as her."

"Did he ever find out it was you?"

"No. Not that I know of."

"That was nice of you to do that for her."

"Like I told you before, there wasn't anything we wouldn't do for each other."

He set my phone down and reached over, pushing my hair behind my ear. I yawned and he laughed.

"Am I boring you?"

"Just a little." I grinned.

"Is that so? Well, maybe I need to make things a little more exciting." He rolled me over so I was lying on my stomach as his fingers pushed the fabric of my panties to the side and he dipped them inside me.

"Is this better?"

"Oh yes," I moaned in excitement.

****

We spent the next few days touring the wineries and taking in everything Napa Valley had to offer. On our last night there, I secretly signed us up for a cooking lesson. After all, Alex did drag me golfing, which I had never done before. But I played nice and pretended that I was interested when I really wasn't. I accidentally hit him with the club, which was his fault for standing so close. Even though I hit him, that was my first hole-in-one and I jumped up and down, screaming with excitement as he held his arm. Oops.

The next morning, we checked out and started our drive back to Malibu. I was flipping through the radio stations when "Don't Look Back in Anger" started to play on the radio.

"Sing with me." I smiled as I held up my phone.

We sang loudly as I recorded us. When the song ended, I held up my hand to him for a high five.

"I sent the video to your phone so you'll never forget me."

"Thanks." He smiled. "But I don't think I could ever forget you."

I looked at him and then turned to look out the passenger window. After about thirty minutes of silence, Alex spoke.

"I have to go out of town tomorrow for a couple of days. But when I get back, I thought maybe we could hit the golf course. What do you say?"

"Where are you going?"

"To Seattle. I'm meeting with a friend of mine. We are looking into opening a hotel together."

"Have fun. I hope it rains." I smiled.

He laughed. "It's Seattle. I'm sure it will be raining."

"I'll play golf with you again and I promise I won't hit you with the club or score a hole in one, so you won't feel emasculated."

He looked over at me and frowned. "I didn't feel emasculated."

"Yes you did!" I laughed. "The look on your face was priceless when I made that shot."

"It was luck, Emerson. Pure luck!"

"Okay, smarty pants. We'll see if that luck continues." I smirked.

****

Alex

The next morning, I softly kissed Emerson's head before tiptoeing out of her room so I didn't wake her up. But I did the minute my hand gripped the doorknob.

"Sneaking off like you did the walk the shame or something, Parker," she whispered with a smile on her face and her eyes still shut.

I turned and walked back to the bed, sitting down next to her and softly stroking her hair.

"No. I didn't want to wake you. I have to leave for Seattle now."

"Okay. Make sure to dance in the rain while you're there." She opened her eyes and looked up at me.

"I will." A smile graced my face as I brushed my lips against hers and walked out of the room.

I sighed as I grabbed my suitcase and headed to the Bentley. Something didn't feel right. I hated leaving her. The times we'd spent together since she arrived had been the greatest times of my life. I shook my head as I climbed in the back seat.

"Everything okay, Alex?" Phillip asked.

"I'm not sure, Phillip."

"Are you feeling okay?"

"Health wise, yes."

He shot me a look from the rearview mirror and gently smiled at me.

When the plane touched down in Seattle, it was raining. I couldn't help but smile as I stepped off the plane. Once I arrived at Hotel Luxe, my room was ready and, as soon as I got settled, I met Simon for lunch down in the restaurant.

"Good to see you, Alex," he spoke as we shook hands.

"Good to see you too, Simon."

We took our seats at a quiet table in the corner and talked business first.

"What's wrong with you? You seem off today."

"Nothing. It's nothing."

"Come on, Alex. We've been friends for years. There isn't anything you can't tell me. I can see something is bothering you."

"It's just this girl that's staying at my house. She's really gotten to me." I took a drink of my scotch.

His eyebrow raised as he looked at me in silence for a moment. "A girl is staying with you?"

"You know my friend Adam?"

"Yeah."

"It's his sister."

"Ouch. That's tough. How long have you known her?"

"It's been almost two months and she's so different from anyone I'd ever met. She's mouthy, defiant, lives life irresponsibly. She travels the world for her twin sister, who died in a car accident eight years ago."

"Huh?"

"It's a long story."

He picked up his drink and pointed at me. "It sounds like to me that you really care for this girl."

"I do. I care for her a lot. More than I should. If I would have known this was going to happen, I wouldn't have let Adam talk me into letting her stay with me."

"How would you have known? Are you only thinking with your dick?"

I smirked. "No."

"So you haven't slept with her?"

"Oh, I have. Multiple times. More times than I should have because each time we have sex, it just gets better and better."

"Well, my friend, it sounds like the two of you have a special connection. Have you told her how you feel?"

I took another sip of my scotch. "God no. I couldn't. Besides, it doesn't matter anyway."

"Why?" He frowned.

"Because she's leaving California in another month."

"To go where?"

"I have no clue. All I know is that she won't stay in California. It holds too many bad memories for her."

"Oh. Then make her see that she can start over with new and good memories. If you're really serious about her, make her see that living in California with you can be the best thing for her. Go after what you want, Alex. I shouldn't have to tell you that."

I sighed. "I know, Simon. But with her, it won't be that simple. She's a very complicated woman."

We finished our business meeting and lunch and Simon had to leave to get back to the office.

"I'll make the amendments in the proposal and we'll get together tomorrow to look over it one last time before you head back home. I'll be in touch, man. It was good seeing you."

"Thanks, Simon. It was good seeing you too. Thanks for listening."

"No problem. That's what friends are for." As he began to walk away, he pointed at me. "Remember, if you want something bad enough, you have to fight for it."

Upon entering my suite, I sat down and opened up my laptop to check my emails and do some work. I would normally meet up with other friends, hit a bar, drink, and maybe pick up a girl for sex. But today, I wasn't interested in any of that. The only girl I couldn't stop thinking about was Emerson. She was in my head all the time and I found myself missing her already. I missed that damn sassy mouth of hers. As I was on my laptop, I pulled up the definition of love again. Everything about that definition held true for me where Emerson was concerned. I would do anything for her and everything to make her happy. Maybe Simon was right and I needed to make her see that staying in California with me was what was best for her. I wasn't ready to let her go in a month's time. Fuck, I didn't want to ever let her go.

I forgot to take my blood pressure medication this morning so I got up off the couch and went into my bag. They weren't there. It suddenly hit me that I forgot to grab them off my nightstand. Shit. I was so focused on not wanting to leave Emerson that I forgot them. I had an idea.

Chapter 24

Emerson

I was in the kitchen preparing dinner for myself so that I would have time to do some laps in the pool before I ate. Alex had been gone for hours and I couldn't quite get a grip on myself. I felt off. It wasn't any different than him being at the office, but knowing that he wasn't going to be coming home for a couple of nights bothered me. I was already missing him and his uptight attitude. I never missed anyone except Emily, Adam, and my parents. I was getting too close to Alex and letting him into the deepest part of my soul. As I was preparing the chicken, Phillip walked into the kitchen.

"Hey, Phillip. What are you doing here?"

"Excuse me, Emerson, but I need you to go pack a bag and come with me."

I laughed. "Where are we going?" I asked as I continued prepping the chicken.

"To the airport. It seems that Mr. Parker forgot his blood pressure medication and he needs you to bring it to him."

I looked up at him in disbelief. "He's in Seattle. He wants me to fly all the way to Seattle to bring him his medication?"

"Yes. The private jet is fueled and waiting for you. When you arrive in Seattle, there will be someone waiting for you with a car to take you to the hotel."

"You're serious, aren't you?"

"Yes. I am." He smiled.

At that moment, Jenna walked into the kitchen.

"Jenna, could you please put the chicken in refrigerator. I'm being summoned by His Majesty."

"Huh?" She gave me a strange look. "He's in Seattle. Isn't he?"

"Yes, and he forgot his medication, so he needs me to bring it to him."

She laughed and shook her head. "Have fun in Seattle."

I sighed as I went to my bedroom. The good thing was that I was already semi-packed from Napa. I took out my old clothes, packed some new ones, and headed to the airport with Phillip. Arriving to the hotel, I took the elevator up to the top floor to the Presidential Suite. As I knocked on the door, I said, "Room service," and held up Alex's bottle of pills. The door opened and he stood there with a smile on his face.

"Your pills all the way from California, Your Majesty." I took a bow.

He stood there with his hands on his hips and his head tilted. "Really, Emerson?"

I laughed as I stepped inside. "How could you forget your pills, Parker?"

"I just did. Thank you for bringing them to me."

"Like I had a choice?" I smiled as I walked around, checking out how amazing his suite was.

"Not really. But aren't you happy to be here in Seattle? It was raining earlier and it's supposed to rain again tomorrow." He smirked.

"Oh, well, in that case, I'm extremely happy to be here. Thank you. But I will have you know that I was in the middle of making a spectacular meal for myself when Phillip dropped by."

He walked over to me and placed his hand on my cheek, sending my panties into a soaking wet frenzy. "You can make it when we get home."

I froze for a moment, my heart suddenly racing. The way he said "when we get home" sparked a feeling inside me that freaked me out. I hadn't had a "home" since my parents and Emily died. Even when Adam sold the house and I moved in with him, it wasn't home.

"What's wrong?" Alex asked.

I gave him a small smile. "Nothing. It's just the way you said that."

"Said what?"

"'When we get home.' That's your home, Alex. Not mine."

"It's yours too as long as you're staying there," he spoke softly.

I placed my hand on his chest. "Thank you, Alex. That's very sweet of you, but a home isn't somewhere temporary."

He took hold of my hand. "Let's not talk about this anymore. Let's go do something."

"What do you want to do?" I asked.

"You pick. I'll do whatever you want to." He softly smiled.

"I picked just about everything we did in Napa, so it's your turn."

"Fine. Give me a second. I'll be right back. Did you pack a dress?"

"No. I didn't think I'd be needing one."

"Okay. After I make this call, we'll go buy you one."

"Where are we going?" I asked.

"You'll see. I'll be right back."

My stomach was a-flutter at the thought of what he had planned. A few moments later, he walked back into the room with a smile on his face.

"Are you ready to go shopping?"

"Are you going to tell me where we're going?"

"I am taking you on a moonlight dinner cruise."

"Fancy, Parker." My lips gave way to a big smile.

****

As I was in the dressing room at Saks, Alex waited outside in an oversized chair. When I walked out in a short, red, sleeveless dress, he looked at me.

"What do you think?"

"It's alright, but I think you can do better."

"Perfect." I grinned. "This is the one I'll take," I spoke to the saleswoman as I looked at myself in the mirror. "I'm just going to wear it out, so could you please remove the price tag?"

"Certainly, miss," she replied.

"Are you wearing those shoes with that dress?" Alex asked.

I looked down at my flip-flops and sighed.

"No worries. I have the perfect shoes to go with the dress. What size are you?"

"Size 7," I replied.

Alex sat there with a grin on his face.

"What?"

He got up from the chair and walked over to me. Leaning close to my ear, he whispered, "I knew you'd pick that dress if I said I didn't like it. But guess what?" He grinned.

"What?"

"I really do like it and I think it looks beautiful on you."

"Jerk!" I lightly smacked his chest.

He laughed and the saleswoman brought me a nice pair of red heels that matched the dress perfectly.

Stepping onto the boat, I noticed Alex and I were the only ones on it.

"Is it just us?"

"Yep."

"How did you do this on such short notice?" I asked as he grabbed my hand and led me up to the upper deck where a table for two covered in white linens sat.

"I arranged it earlier. When I made the call, it was to let the captain know what time we'd be arriving."

"Hmm." I smiled. "And what if I wanted to do something else?"

"We still would have ended up here." He winked.

After an amazing dinner under the moonlight, a bottle of champagne, and a lot of talk, we headed back to the hotel. The minute we stepped into the room, Alex came up from behind, lightly grasped my shoulders, and began softly kissing my neck. When I let out a light moan, his fingers began to unzip my dress. This man always unraveled me to the point where I couldn't breathe. The way his hands manipulated my body and the way his mouth devoured me always left me inebriated. Letting my dress fall to the ground, his hands caressed my breasts.

"I want you so bad," he whispered.

I turned around and our mouths met. Our tongues tangled in passion and my skin was set on fire. His fingers slowly traveled down my torso until they reached the fabric of my panties. In one swoop, they were down and his fingers explored me.

"You love this. Don't you?"

"Yes," I breathed out.

"You're always so wet and delicious. I can't stop myself when you're around."

My hands reached for his pants. Feeling the big bulge in front, I stroked him through the fabric. He hissed. My hands reached up and began unbuttoning his shirt. Sliding it off his shoulders, I gripped his muscular arms. Arms that made me feel safe. Arms that held me at night after sex. Pulling his fingers out, his tongue slid down the front of me, stopping at each breast first, sucking my hardened nipples before making his way down the fiery aching spot that desperately needed him. Getting down on his knees, he started with my inner thigh, making tiny circles around it until he reached my slick opening. A low moan escaped his chest as he tasted the pleasure that was made because of him.

"I can't wait anymore, baby." He stood, picked me up and carried me to the table that sat twelve. Facing the table, and with him standing behind me, he took down his pants and threw them to the side. He leaned into me, resting his hard cock on the small of my back. Lightly grabbing my hair, he pulled my head back.

"Are you ready?" he whispered.

"I'm always ready."

"Jesus, Emerson," he spoke, winded as he thrust inside me, burying himself deep inside my soul.

I moaned loudly, which caused his thrusting to increase in speed. He was pounding into me like he never had before. Suddenly, he pulled out and turned me around, lifting me up so I was sitting on the edge of the table. Wrapping my legs around his waist, he thrust into me a few times and then laid me on my back so I was stretched out on the table. He climbed on top and hovered over me while he brushed the strands of hair from my face, his eyes staring into mine. Once again, he thrust into me, slow and smooth before bringing his lips to mine. It wasn't long before his rhythmic movement brought me to an amazing orgasm, panting out his name as he pushed one last time inside and held himself there, filling me with his come.

“Are you okay?” He smiled.

I lay there, underneath him, panting and trying to catch my breath.

“Yep. I’m good. I mean, great. I mean, fuck, Alex, what was that?”

He chuckled as he kissed my lips.

“I’m going to assume you thoroughly enjoyed it?”

“Enjoyed it is way too mild of a statement. That was mind-blowing. The type of mind-blowing sex that leaves your body craving for more every second of every day. The kind that stays with you and on your mind 24/7. The kind that one doesn’t forget so easily.”

The grin on his face grew wide as he placed his hand on my cheek.

“Good. I’ll make you a deal. Any time your body is craving that mind-blowing sex, I’m more than willing and happy to fulfill your body’s needs.”

I placed my hand on his chest. “You are way too kind, Parker. My body thanks you.”

Laughing, he kissed me one more time before climbing off of me and helping me up.

Chapter 25

Emerson

I awoke wrapped in Alex's arms. The sheets tangled around us from the second round of mind-blowing sex we had. I lay there and listened to the drops of rain softly hit the railing of the balcony. I quietly climbed out of bed, slipped on my robe, and went out onto the balcony, staring at the city of Seattle. Being here with Alex was something I hadn't planned on. Things were intense between us. Feelings and emotions I never experienced before crept in and left me dazed and confused. My stomach started to flutter every time he was around. What the fuck was that about? I mentioned on more than one occasion how his scent drove me wild. But it was getting extreme. The moment I would catch a whiff of him, my pheromones took over and the ache below became more unbearable than the previous time.

"Can't sleep?" I heard Alex say as he stepped out onto the balcony and wrapped his arms around my waist while laying his chin on my shoulder.

"I can sleep. I just woke up and heard the rain, so I thought I'd come out here for a while. I didn't mean to wake you." I placed my hands on his arms.

He felt good. Too good. Dangerously good. No one had ever made me feel this good before.

"You didn't wake me." His lips pressed into the side of my head.

"If I didn't wake you, then why are you up?"

"Because I rolled over and I didn't feel you next to me."

"So I did wake you up?"

He laughed. "Fine. You woke me up."

"Sorry," I whispered.

"Don't be. You can wake me up anytime you want."

There was something I didn't tell him. Something that happened earlier. I got a call from Adam and his work was almost finished in Tennessee. He'd be home next week, we'd have our talk, and then I'd leave; move on to the next adventure.

"Adam called me this morning."

"How is he?" Alex asked.

"He'll be home next week."

"Really? I thought he had three more weeks there."

"He wrapped up early."

"I see." He let go of me and went back inside the room. I followed.

"What's wrong?"

"Nothing. It's three in the morning. We really should get some sleep."

I climbed in on my side and Alex climbed in on his. He turned on his side, his eyes staring into mine. His lips softly brushed against mine.

"Get some sleep, Emerson."

"You too, Parker." I smiled as I ran my finger over his lips.

He turned on his back and I snuggled tightly against him.

****

Alex

I lay there, holding Emerson as tight as I could. Her leg was wrapped around me and her head lay on my chest. Adam would be home next week, and then, before I knew it, Emerson would leave. The thought of her leaving bothered me more than it should have. We'd grown so close and I had shared parts of my life with her. I didn't want her to leave California. It had only been two months since I'd first met her, but in some unexplainable way, she had become a huge part of my life in such a short period of time, and I wasn't ready to let her go. Fuck. I was going to do everything I could to make her stay.

****

I had room service delivered for us since we had barely slept. Emerson had just gotten out of the shower when our breakfast arrived.

"Thank God. I'm starving." She smiled as she walked past me and smacked my ass.

"Really?"

"Really what?" she asked as she picked up a piece of toast and bit into it.

"You had to smack my ass when you walked by?"

She giggled. "Mhmm, and what a fine ass it is."

I sighed as I sat down at the table.

"Did you wipe down the table?" she asked.

"Umm. No. Why would I?"

"Have you forgotten that we had sex on this table?"

"Trust me. I haven't forgotten." I got up, took my plate, and walked down to the other end of the table. Are you coming?" I raised a brow at her.

She picked up her plate and sat down across from me.

"Your hot ass didn't touch this area down here, so we're good." I smiled.

"Gotcha." She winked.

"Start thinking about what you want to do after my meeting."

"I would love to go to the zoo. There's one only a few miles from here."

"The zoo? Really?"

"Yes, the zoo. Do you have a problem with the zoo, Parker?"

"No. I haven't been to the zoo since I was a small child and my nanny took me."

"Your nanny? Why am I not surprised?" She laughed.

"I'll have you know that my nanny was one of the best."

"I'm sure she was. Can I tell you how honored I am, Your Majesty, to be the second person ever to explore the zoo with you." She took a bow.

I sighed. "Why do you do that?"

The grin on her face widened. "Because I know it pisses you off."

"Are you trying to raise my blood pressure, Emerson?"

"No," she spoke with a twisted face. "Don't forget to take your pill." She smacked my hand as I reached for the salt shaker.

"A little bit of salt won't kill me, but a little bit of Emerson just might." I winked.

"Haha. Very funny, Parker."

I got up from the table, grabbed my suit coat, and kissed Emerson on the top of her head. "I have to get to my meeting. When I return, we will go to the zoo."

Chapter 26

Emerson

I finished getting ready, and while I was waiting for Alex to return from his meeting, I poured myself a glass of wine and sat out on the balcony. Leaving Alex was probably going to be the hardest thing I'd ever done, but he'd be okay and so would I. Never stay in one place too long.

I had just stepped inside the room when the door opened and Alex walked in.

"How did your meeting go?"

"It went great. Are you ready?" He asked as he kissed my lips.

"Yes."

"Great. Just give me a second to go change," he spoke as he walked into the bedroom.

As we walked through the zoo, Alex had a smile on his face. He was enjoying seeing the animals and I found it to be quite a turn-on.

"OMG! It's the lemurs. It's King Julian!" I exclaimed.

"Who?" he asked.

I gave him a perplexed look. "King Julian. You know, from *Madagascar*?"

He slowly shook his head. "From what?"

"You have never seen *Madagascar*?" I asked in shock.

"I have no clue what *Madagascar* or King Julian is."

I placed my hands on each side of his face. "You have lived a very deprived and boring life, Parker."

He chuckled and hooked his arm around me.

After a fun day at the zoo, I was feeling pretty tired so I asked Alex if we could have dinner back in our room. Once we made it back, he handed me the room service menu and asked what I wanted while he poured us some wine.

"I want a pizza."

"Pizza? You don't want a nice steak, or maybe some fish?"

Climbing on the bed, I shook my head. "Nope. You order that for yourself if you want, but I'm having pizza."

"Okay. Then we'll both have pizza. What do you want on it?"

"Anything but anchovies. You pick." I smiled.

"How about pepperoni, mushrooms, and green peppers?"

"Sounds good to me. Could you also order some of that lemon cheesecake I saw on the menu?"

"Of course." He grinned.

He placed the order for dinner and I patted his side of the bed. He smiled as he sat down next to me.

"Don't you think we should wait to have sex after the pizza comes? I would hate to be in the middle of it and there's a knock on the door."

"We aren't having sex, Parker. We're going to watch *Madagascar.*"

"Seriously?" His playful look turned serious.

"Yes. It's such a cute movie. You need to let out the inner child in you. Now make yourself comfy." I pointed the remote to the TV and searched for *Madagascar* on the pay channels.

We sat on the bed, our backs propped up against pillows while we ate pizza, drank wine, and laughed at *Madagascar*. Every time I looked over at Alex, I could tell he was enjoying it. I shoulder bumped him and he looked over at me.

"What?"

"You're loving King Julian." I smiled.

"Actually, the penguins are my favorite."

"Yeah. They're pretty cool but King Julian rules!"

"King Julian is great but I'm a sucker for the penguins." He grinned.

When the movie was over, Alex noticed there was a second one.

"Rent the second one," he spoke.

"Don't you think we should get some sleep since we're leaving in the morning?"

"Go ahead and lie down, then, but I'm going to watch the second movie."

"And sex?" I asked as I ran my finger down his chest.

"Sex can wait, Emerson. The penguins can't."

I sighed. I think I had just created a *Madagascar* monster. I set my wine glass on the nightstand and rolled over, secretly smiling while I listened to him laugh as he watched *Madagascar 2.*

****

Alex

When we arrived home, I went up to my office and started to do some much needed work. I had been taking way too much time away from my company and, surprisingly, it didn't fall apart. As I was sitting at my desk, the reality of Adam coming home this week set in and, suddenly, my mood changed. After a couple of hours, I went downstairs and saw Emerson doing laps in the pool.

"I'm going to the office for a while. I'll see you later."

"Okay. I'll cook us dinner."

I gave her a nod and drove myself to a bar instead of the office. I just needed to think over a couple of drinks and I couldn't do that with Emerson in the house.

"What can I get you, friend?" the bartender named Alan asked.

"Scotch on the rocks. Make it a double."

"Coming right up."

He poured the scotch and set the glass down in front of me. I drank it faster than he set it down.

"Another," I said.

"You okay, man? You slammed that pretty fast."

"Actually, I'm not okay. The woman I'm in love with is going to be leaving California soon and I don't think there's a damn thing I can do to stop her."

"Sorry to hear that. Have you told her that you love her?"

"Not yet, and even if I did, it wouldn't matter. She hates it here. This place holds too many bad memories for her."

He handed me another glass of scotch. "Maybe you can show her what the good memories used to be. Make her forget about the bad," he spoke.

"She lost her parents and twin sister in an accident several years ago. She'll never be able to forget that. Pour me another." I threw a hundred-dollar bill on the counter.

"Nah. That would be hard to forget. I'm sorry, bro, but before that, there had to be good memories."

I kept drinking and, before I knew it, Alan cut me off.

"Did you drive here?" he asked.

"Yes."

"Well, you aren't driving home. Can I call someone for you?"

"No."

"Then I'm calling you a cab."

"No. Call Phillip. His number is in my phone." I slid my phone to him.

About a half hour had passed, and as I laid my head down on the bar, I felt a hand on my shoulder.

"What the hell are you doing, Parker?"

Lifting my head, I looked up to see Emerson standing next to me.

"I thought I told you to call Phillip?" I drunkenly spoke to Alan.

"He didn't answer and she kept calling. You need to go home, friend, and sleep the alcohol off."

"Let's go, Alex." She grabbed my arm and helped me up.

As I stumbled out the door, Emerson began to yell at me.

"I thought you were going to the office. I made this nice dinner for us. I sat there alone, waiting for you to come home, and you were sitting in this bar getting drunk. Why?"

I didn't say a word as she shoved me into the passenger seat of Adam's car.

"I swear to God, Parker, if you puke in this car, you're buying Adam a new one."

I moaned as I lay my head against the window and she drove me home. She opened the door and grabbed my arm.

"Come on. Give me a little help here, Parker. I may be strong, but I'm not strong enough to hold up your dumb drunk ass."

"I'm going to be sick."

"Not on me you're not. You are to wait until we get into the house. If you throw up on me, you're buying me all new clothes and I'll make sure they're high end designer and cost you thousands of dollars. No, make that millions."

I stumbled through the door and she took me to the bathroom off the foyer.

"There. Now you can throw up, you stupid man."

Once I was done, I sat up against the wall as she wiped my mouth with a wash cloth.

"Can you get up the stairs?" she asked in irritation.

I moaned as I fell over.

"I guess that's a no."

She helped me up and took me to her room, stripped me naked, and helped me into bed. As she climbed in next to me, the last words I remember her saying were, "Throw up on me and I'll stab you in your sleep." I silently smiled because her mouth never stopped and I loved it.

Chapter 27

Emerson

It was the end of the week and Adam was due home today. Alex and I never talked about that night he got drunk. He wouldn't talk about it and had been irritable all week long. We didn't have sex and I barely saw him. He reverted back to staying late at the office and when I would text him and ask when he was coming home, he would just reply "soon."

I pulled out my map and laid it across my bed to make my plan for my next move. With Alex's behavior, he was making it easier for me to leave. What happened to the man back in Napa and Seattle? Something went seriously wrong and I wanted to know what it was. The night he left and told me he was going to the office, nothing had happened, and I thought things were good between us. He was shutting me out again and it hurt me. It hurt me right down to the very core of my soul. I thought a lot about things and needed to put my mind to rest and concentrate on where I was going to go next. I still couldn't help but be bothered that my money was almost gone. Something wasn't right because I didn't live to the extreme. I was very careful with what I spent.

As I was looking over my map, I glanced at my phone and it was seven p.m. Just as I diverted my eyes back to the map, my phone rang and it was Adam.

"Hey, Adam."

"Hey, Em. I wanted to let you know that I'm on my way over. I should be there in about ten minutes. I can't wait to see you, sis."

"I can't wait to see you either."

I took in a deep breath and folded up my map. As I was on my way to the kitchen, the front door opened and Alex walked in.

"Impeccable timing, Parker," I spoke as I continued walking.

"What do you mean?" He followed me into the kitchen and set his brief case down.

"Adam should be here in about ten minutes. Make sure to have a bottle of wine ready to pour for me. You and he will have to get your own."

****

Alex

I'd been a real bastard to Emerson all week. The reason? I couldn't stand the thought of her leaving. If I distanced myself from her and put everything we had done and been through behind us, it would be easier on me when she left. It was wrong, I know. But it was the way I dealt with things. I loved her so damn much and it was killing me to know that she wouldn't be around much longer. I wanted to talk to her about that night, but I couldn't. It was a lost cause. I would have confessed my feelings to her and been left there standing like an idiot. If she loved me, she would stay. Now, Adam was on his way over and I wasn't sure how that was going to go. Since he never talked about his family, I would bet my life that his views were completely different from Emerson's and there was going be a lot of arguing. I was glad I came home from the office early. This reunion was going to be interesting.

I went down to the wine cellar, grabbed a bottle of Pinot, and brought it upstairs.

"Here's your bottle."

"Thanks." She smiled.

She took out the corkscrew and attempted to open the bottle. I noticed her hands were shaking. Placing my hands around hers, I spoke, "Let me open that for you."

She let go of the bottle and reached up and grabbed a glass from the cabinet, dropping it to the floor.

"Fuck!" she yelled.

This wasn't like her. "Emerson, don't touch the glass. You'll cut yourself."

"I'm sorry. I'll buy you another glass."

"Fuck the glass. What is wrong with you?" I asked as I walked over to her. "Are you that nervous to talk to your brother?"

"I don't know. Maybe I am. These conversations never go well with him. It's the same thing over and over again, like a vicious, never-ending cycle."

"Maybe this time will be different," I spoke as I bent down to clean up the glass.

"Doubt it."

The doorbell rang and she stiffened up. I couldn't help myself. I kissed her head and gave her a hug before sending her into the war zone.

****

Emerson

I was happy to see my brother, but I was not looking forward to our conversation. The moment I saw him, I stood there for a moment as tears filled my eyes. It had been a long time.

"Hey, sis." He smiled as he held out his arms.

I ran to him and hugged him tight. "It's so good to see you."

"It's good to see you too. Look at you." He slowly shook his head.

"Adam." Alex walked over and shook his hand.

"Alex." He smiled. "Thanks for looking after my sister."

I studied the look on Alex's face. He simply smiled and gave Adam a nod. "Can I get you a drink?"

"Bourbon would be great. Thank you."

I led Adam into the living room and grabbed my glass of wine, taking a large sip.

"So how was Tennessee?" I asked with a smile.

"It was okay. I got the company up and running again with no problems."

"Good." I laid my head on his shoulder.

Alex handed Adam his drink and I couldn't help but notice the way he stared at me and Alex.

"Have you decided where you're going to settle?" he asked.

Wow. Let's just cut right to the chase.

"No. I need to talk to you about the money situation first. I really don't understand how it's almost gone."

"That's because you were off on your own little adventure without a care in the world."

I took in a deep breath because, suddenly, the air became a whole lot thicker.

"I'll leave you two alone," Alex spoke as he began to walk away.

"PARKER, SIT!" I commanded in a harsh voice.

"Excuse me?"

"You heard me. Sit down!" I pointed at the chair and glared at him.

He took a seat in the wing-backed chair and looked at Adam.

"You let her talk to you like that, man?"

Alex shrugged and Adam got up from the couch.

"So why don't the two of you tell me what's going on here."

"Nothing," Alex responded.

"Adam." I tried my hold my composure. "You brought me back to talk about me and my, as you call them, 'adventures.' This is about me and you. Not about me and Alex."

Adam gave me a stern look as he took a sip of his bourbon. His tone changed as he sat down next to me on the couch and took hold of my hands.

"Listen, Em. You spent the last eight years gallivanting around the world and now it's time for you to settle down and make a place your home. You can't keep going on like this. It isn't healthy and it's irresponsible."

"Why is it irresponsible? Because I chose to see the world instead of being held up in a stuffy office working a 9-5 job that I hate?"

"I don't hate my job. You're living off our dead parents' money, sis."

"I've had a few jobs over the years. Hell, I worked at Billy's ranch, for God sakes."

"Who's Billy?" he asked. "Oh wait, the bull rider."

I tilted my head and narrowed my eye. "No. That was Austin in Montana."

"You were in Montana?" Alex asked as he cocked his head.

I held my hand up to him.

"You never mentioned Montana," he spoke.

"It wasn't worth mentioning. Anyway, Billy was the cowboy from Texas."

"That's right. The most recent one. The reason you needed to leave Texas."

I sighed as I got up from the couch and took my glass of wine with me.

"That money is mine to do whatever I wanted to do with it. You sure didn't give me this much hell when I left in the first place."

"You know why I didn't?" Adam spoke with a raised voice. "Because I thought it was temporary. I didn't think you'd be gone for eight fucking years!"

"I told you that I wasn't coming back here!"

"You had everything going for you. You healed an arm that the doctor's said you'd probably never be able to use again. You broke three records at Nationals. You had the best universities kissing your ass, hoping you'd pick them. You could have made something of yourself, but instead, you chose to run. Ran away from what happened here, from me, your friends, and everything that made you who you are."

"That's not true," I spoke as tears filled my eyes.

"If it's not true, then explain it to me!" he yelled.

"I don't have to explain anything to you! I'm an adult!"

"You can't explain it to me because you've been running for so long, you don't even know why anymore."

"I'm doing it for Emily. This is what we always dreamed of and talked about since we were kids."

"You don't think I know that!" Adam got up from the couch. "The two of you were always talking about going somewhere. It was a pipe dream the two of you had."

I gulped when he said that. "How dare you." I pointed my finger at him.

Chapter 28

Emerson

I walked over to the table and poured another glass of wine. The anger inside me was at a level I never knew existed.

"Admit it, Emerson. You're running and chasing something that can never be found." His voice softened.

I turned away as I wiped the tears that fell from my eyes. I looked at Alex as he sat there with a saddened look on his face.

"I'm not running. I'm doing what me and Emily always talked about. I was on death's door!" I whipped myself around and glared at Adam. "I actually died and then came back and spent three months in a coma. I'll never get those three months of my life back and I don't know when the next accident will happen, so excuse me, big brother, for wanting to see what I always dreamed of before I die."

"That's not the reason, Em, and you know it. Have you visited Mom's, Dad's and Emily's graves yet?"

"That's none of your business," I spoke through gritted teeth.

"You haven't." He shook his head and looked at Alex. "Did she tell you that she never visited their graves, ever?!"

"No. I wasn't aware of that," Alex responded.

"You buried them when I was lying in a hospital bed fighting for my life," I yelled.

"I had no choice! It had to be done and I didn't know if you would ever wake up. Do you have any idea how hard it was to bury three members of my family at the same time and to maybe have to bury a fourth? Do you even care how I felt?!"

"I know that must have been hard on you and I'm sorry."

"You're sorry? I had to take a year off of college to take care of you. I sat by your bedside every fucking day begging you to wake up because the thought of losing the only person I had left killed me. Then, when you finally woke up, I took care of you. I was there for you every night while you cried yourself to sleep and asked God why he didn't just take you. I supported you and provided for you so you could get better and move on with your life. And what's the first thing you do? You take off and leave me here alone. You weren't the only one who lost Mom, Dad, and Emily! I lost them too! They were just as much my family as they were yours! I needed you here for support and you didn't care."

"I never asked you to take care of me," I cried.

"You didn't have to. You're my sister and I'm your brother. It was my obligation to our parents and sister to make sure you came through everything that happened okay. But I failed the day you walked out that door and never looked back. Because you know what, Em? You're not okay and you won't be until you accept their deaths."

"I have accepted it!" I screamed.

Alex got up from his chair and attempted to wrap his arms around me. I pushed him away. "Don't."

"If you accepted it, then why haven't you gone to their graves? Why do you keep running from this place? You had just as many good memories here as bad. Shit happens, Em. People die. It's life. I lost you too that day and I'm sorry that I couldn't bring you back."

I fell to my knees because I couldn't take it anymore, and it was at that moment that I realized my brother's anger and attitude were because he felt as if he'd failed me. In reality, though, I was the one who had failed him.

"Adam, I'm—"

"Save it, Em. I need you to sign these papers." He threw them on the table. "I lied to you. You have money left, and as soon as you sign those papers, it's all yours. I am no longer responsible for your finances. I wanted you to see that it was time for you to settle down and stop running from the past. But obviously, you aren't ever going to stop running until something happens to you and I won't be there to pick up the pieces." He turned and walked out of the living room. A few moments later, the slamming of the front door startled me.

I sat on the floor, crying and enraged by everything that had just happened. Alex walked over to me and placed his hand on my shoulder.

"Emerson."

"Don't touch me!" I yelled as I stood up. "You lost that right when you shut me out this past week."

"Calm down." He grabbed my arms and pulled me into him, holding me so tight that I could barely breathe.

I tried to loosen myself from his grip, but couldn't. Finally, I gave up and just sank to the ground with him as I held on to him for dear life.

****

Alex

Seeing her in so much pain broke my heart into a million pieces. She needed me and I was going to be there for her. I put all my thoughts and the shit that had happened aside because I loved her and I was going to see that she got through this. I picked her up and carried her to her bedroom. As I gently laid her on the bed, she grabbed my hand.

"Please stay," she begged.

"Of course."

I climbed in next to her and wrapped my arms around her. She didn't want to talk and I respected that. She didn't want to be alone and I didn't want to leave her alone. After falling asleep for a couple of hours, I awoke to Emerson coming out of the bathroom in her nightshirt.

"How are you?" I asked as I sat up.

"I don't know. God, Alex, so much shit was revealed tonight. Things Adam never told me."

"I know." I held out my hand to her.

She placed her hand in mine and crawled back into bed.

"Are you hungry?" I asked.

"Kind of. You?"

"Yeah. I am. How about a pizza?"

She gave me a small smile. "Sounds good."

We walked to the kitchen and I placed the order for the pizza while Emerson poured us each a glass of wine. Her eyes were swollen and she looked tired. I just wanted to whisk her away from all of this. I saw Emerson's point, but I also understood Adam's. We took a seat outside on the patio.

"How do you feel about Adam lying to you about your money situation?"

She looked up at me with her sad eyes. "I'm mad, but I get why he did it."

"He wants his sister back, Em."

She gave me a small smile. "That's the first time you've called me that."

"It is. Isn't it?" I tilted my head at her.

I heard the doorbell ring and, when I got up, Emerson took hold of my hand.

"Bring the pizza down to the beach. I want to eat down there by the water."

"In the sand?" I arched my brow.

"Yeah. In the sand."

I nodded my head and walked inside. After I paid for the pizza, I took the box down to the beach and sat down next to Emerson, handing her a slice of pizza.

"I'm sorry for yelling at you earlier," she spoke.

"Don't apologize. You were stressed out and upset."

"I shouldn't have said that to you."

I chuckled. "There were a lot of things you never should have said to me. Like, you were going to break my balls."

She laughed. "I apologized to you for saying that."

"You did, but you also said you wouldn't hesitate to say it again." I smiled as I shoulder bumped her.

"Have you ever really listened closely to the ocean?" she asked with seriousness.

"What do you mean? Oh shit!" I dropped my pizza in the sand. "Now see, if were sitting at the table, this wouldn't be an issue."

"Just grab another piece." She laughed.

Reaching into the box, I grabbed another slice and looked over at her. "What did you mean by that?"

"Just listen for a minute. Do you hear the subtle hissing sound?"

"Actually, I do." I listened carefully. "Why haven't you ever visited your parents' and Emily's graves?"

"The truth?" She looked over at me.

"Always."

"Because if I did, it would mean I would have to say goodbye." She wiped her eye.

I set down my pizza on top of the box and pulled her into me. "Come here." I softly kissed the top of her head. "You never have to say goodbye, Emerson. You told me that Emily is always with you. She was at Nationals with the dove and in Napa when it rained. You asked for a sign and she gave it to you. Visiting their graves won't change that."

"Then why do it?"

"Everyone is different. I visit my father's grave occasionally and make sure the area is kept up. Plus, I feel closer to him when I'm there."

"Were you and your father close?"

"Yes, we were, and we grew closer after my mother left. I don't know. It just gives me a sense of peace. Come on. Let's go back up to the house. I think you're going to need to shower since you're covered in sand. You are only wearing that nightshirt."

"True. Plus, I'm tired. It's been a clusterfuck of a day and I'm ready for it to end."

I helped her up and grabbed the pizza box. Emerson grabbed our glasses and we walked back up to the house.

Chapter 29

Emerson

After setting the glasses on the counter, I walked to my room and Alex followed, walking into the bathroom and starting the shower for me. I took off my nightshirt and stood before him in nothing but my panties. His eyes raked over my body and the need to make love to him intensified. He slowly walked over to me and placed his hand on my cheek while our eyes locked on each other.

"Take a shower with me," I whispered.

His lips gave way to a small smile. "Are you sure?"

"Yes. I need you tonight."

His lips brushed softly against mine for a moment before he stripped out of his clothes. He took my hand, and we stepped into the shower as the warm water ran down us and our lips tightly locked together.

****

As I let out a yawn, I looked over at the clock and saw the time was ten. When I looked to my side, the only sight I saw was the crumpled sheets and the empty pillow where Alex lay and held me last night. I climbed out of bed, slipped my robe on, and followed the smell of fresh brewed coffee to the kitchen, where I found Alex over the stove, making eggs.

"What's this?" I smiled.

He turned his head and looked at me. "Good morning. I was just about to wake your lazy ass up." He snickered.

Pouring a cup of coffee, I smacked him on the arm.

"Umm. Something's burning."

"Shit. The toast!" He turned to the toaster and popped it up.

I laughed as I grabbed a butter knife. "We can always just scrape off the burnt part and then spread thick layers of jelly across it."

"Very funny. I'll just make new."

"It's fine, Alex." I placed my hand on his arm.

Walking into the dining room, I stopped and took note of the pink rose petals scattered all over the table with a beautiful arrangement of different flowers in a crystal vase.

"What's all this?"

"Nothing. Doesn't everyone eat breakfast on a table filled with rose petals?"

"You don't do rose petals. Remember?"

"Why are you making a big deal about it? Just sit down and eat your scrambled eggs and burnt toast." He smirked.

Sitting down with a smile on my face, I began to eat the eggs Alex so graciously prepared for me.

Crunch.

Crunch.

"What the hell, Parker?" Laughing, I spit the eggs back onto the plate.

"What? That was really gross, Emerson."

"Eggs aren't supposed to be crunchy." I dug through the eggs with my fork. "Oh my God, there's shells in here." I looked up at him.

"Oh. I thought I got all those out. Sorry about that." He pushed his plate away. "Go get dressed. We're going out somewhere."

"Where?"

"For a drive."

"Where?"

"I'm not telling you. You'll see when we get there."

"I really don't feel like going anywhere."

He sighed and got up from his seat. Pulling my chair out, he picked me up and threw me over his shoulder.

"What are you doing?! Put me down."

"I told you to go get dressed and you didn't listen, so I'm dressing you myself."

"The hell you are. Put me down." I pounded on his tight ass.

When we reached the bedroom, he walked into my closet, with me still over his shoulder, and pulled a black sundress from the hanger.

"This will do." He set me down and untied my robe. After sliding it off my shoulders, he pulled the sundress over my head. "There. Now do you need me to do your hair and makeup as well?"

"You're such a douchebag, Parker." I smiled as I walked into the bathroom.

"At least I'm not a fucker. You have fifteen minutes, Emerson. I'll be downstairs waiting."

"Did you take your pill?" I yelled before he walked out.

"Yes."

"Good boy."

****

As we were driving, Alex still wouldn't tell me where we were going, but the route was all too familiar to me. Panic started to settle inside me as he made a left turn into a subdivision.

"Alex, what are you doing?" I asked nervously.

He looked over at me and took hold of my hand but didn't say a word.

"Parker. I'm speaking to you. I don't like this. Turn around!"

"Stop, Emerson," he spoke as he pulled into the driveway of my childhood home.

I gulped as I stared at it from the car window. "I will ask you nicely one last time to please take me back to your house. Because if you don't, I swear to God, I'll break your balls."

"There you go again."

"Alex, I'm serious. This isn't funny and I want to leave."

He grabbed both of my hands and stared at me. "Listen to me. I want you to calm down. This was your childhood home and you had wonderful memories here. We're going to go inside and you're going to tell me about those memories. Okay?"

"How the hell are we going to get inside?"

"The realtor will be here shortly. The house is up for sale and I made an appointment to look at it."

I rolled my eyes and sighed. "How did you even know about this house?"

"I talked to Adam this morning."

"Of course you did. Fuck you, Parker. I'm not going inside that house." I opened the car door and ran straight to the backyard. Why? It was a place of comfort.

As I stopped in the middle of the grass, I looked straight ahead by the oak tree that was still there and at the empty spot where the little house used to be that my dad had built for us. He called it "Twins Cottage."

Alex walked up from behind and clasped my shoulders. "What are you staring at?"

"Over there by the oak tree, Emily and I always played in the cottage my dad built for us. It was our own little house. We would have tea parties when we were really little and then, as we grew, we used it as a place to escape from our parents for a while. Emily and I would sit in there for hours and listen to music and talk about the things we were going to do. We had some amazing times in there. I even got my first kiss in there by a boy named Sam. What happened in that cottage, stayed in that cottage." I smiled.

I walked over to the tree and examined the trunk, finding the arrow that I had carved into it. "See this spot right here?"

"Yeah."

"This is where we buried Muffin, our dog. I carved this arrow in the trunk of the tree pointing down so I'd always remember exactly where she was buried."

Alex put his arms around my waist and kissed my head.

"Excuse me," a woman spoke from behind us. "You must be Alex Parker?"

"Yes, and this is Emerson James."

"Nice to meet you both. Come with me and I'll show you around inside."

I took in the deepest breath I ever took in my life before walking through the back door of the house I grew up in. Stepping inside, memories of my parents, Adam, and Emily flooded my mind. Tears started to spring to my eyes.

"As you can see—" the realtor started to speak.

"Excuse me, ma'am, but I just want to look around myself. If I have any questions, I'll let you know."

"Oh," she spoke with an offended tone. "Well then, I'll be sitting in the kitchen."

"Thank you." Alex smiled gently at her.

Chapter 30

Alex

Maybe bringing Emerson back to her childhood home wasn't the brightest idea I'd ever had, but she needed to be reminded of the good times she'd had here. Was it my place to remind her of them? Yes. I felt it was because I loved her and I wanted her pain to stop. She walked up the stairs and I followed her. Opening one of the doors in the hallway, she walked inside the room.

"This was my and Emily's room. My bed sat in that corner over there and Emily's sat in that corner across from me."

"Why did you two share a room? This is a five-bedroom house."

"Because we couldn't stand to be separated."

Jesus. It was all making sense to me now.

"We used to sit on our beds, do our homework, and talk for hours about everything. This wall over here." She pointed. "This is where our map hung and there was a dresser right underneath it where we always kept a black marker sitting on top. My mom would come in our room to put our laundry away and she'd look at the map. She would smile every time she saw another black circle."

She was smiling and her tone of voice was lighter. She was remembering the good times here and I prayed to God this was enough to make her stay in California.

****

Emerson

The memories that resided in this house were just as strong today as when I was younger. Walking out of my bedroom, I headed down the hallway and ran my finger along the slight crack in the molding outside Adam's bedroom door. I laughed.

"I can't believe it's still here."

"What?" Alex asked.

"See this small crack?"

"Yeah."

"That's from Adam's head. When he was sixteen, he went to a friend's party and came home drunk. He missed the door and cracked his head on the molding. My dad took him to the ER and he got four stitches that night. My mom stayed back with us because she was so angry with him."

Alex laughed. "I bet she was."

Taking Alex's hand, we walked downstairs to the living room. "My mom and dad both loved lighthouses." I walked over to the corner where a curio cabinet used to sit. "They collected them and we had a cabinet that sat right here filled with different ones. Some of them lit up and, at night, my mom would turn them on and turn off all the other lights in the room so the only thing we saw were the glowing lights of the lighthouses. They were beautiful and so peaceful. Next to the cabinet hung a painting of the Bass Harbor Lighthouse in Bass Harbor, Maine. My mom talked about this cute little cottage they stayed at while they were there. My dad proposed to her in front of that very lighthouse. She was sitting on the rocks, staring out into the water, while my dad took pictures of her. She said it was the most beautiful place she'd ever been to. My dad got down on one knee on the rock in front of her and asked her to marry him. She said he totally surprised her because they hadn't even talked about marriage. They bought the painting before they left to remind them of how special of a place it was. She said it symbolized their start of a new life together."

"What happened to the painting?" he asked.

"Adam has it in storage somewhere."

Walking to the kitchen, I looked around and could see my mom standing by the stove. It was her favorite room in the house. "My mom cooked here every single night. She was a great cook. Sometimes, I would help her while Emily went to swim in the pool. Speaking of which." I turned to the realtor. "What happened to the pool?"

"The previous owners took it out because they didn't want it." She gave me an odd look. "Do you know this house?"

"Yes. I grew up here."

"Oh," she spoke with surprise.

Alex walked over to where I was standing and put his arm around me.

"We're looking to possibly start our own family in this house. Isn't that right, baby?"

"Umm. Yes. Yes, we are."

"Excellent!" The realtor smiled.

Her phone rang and she looked at it. "Excuse me. I need to take this call," she spoke as she walked out of the room.

I looked out the window at the spot where the pool used to be. "Who the hell lives in California and doesn't want a pool?"

"Obviously fools." Alex chuckled.

I turned and looked at Alex with a smile on my face. "I have to see if it's still there. Come on." I grabbed his hand and led him through kitchen, through the foyer, out the front door, and onto the porch. I looked in the corner and knelt down, placing my hand on the small handprint that my dad made the three of us do when he built the new porch.

"This is my handprint. This one is Emily's and this is Adam's."

"How old were you?"

"We were six and Adam was ten. I remember the day we did this. My dad said that we'd always be a permanent part of this house now that our handprints were here. He said no matter what life threw at us, we'd always have this house and the memories we made here. Oh my God, Alex. I just remembered all that."

He put his arm around me and pulled me into him. "That's good, Emerson. Your dad sounds like he was a wise man."

"He was."

Suddenly, out of nowhere, the sky opened up and let the rain fall down.

"What the fuck?" Alex said as he stood up.

A smile splayed across my face as I ran out onto the grass and held my arms up. When I threw my head back, the rain fell upon my face. "They're here with us." I smiled as I turned in a circle.

"What the heck is going on?" the realtor spoke. "They weren't calling for rain today."

"It's only temporary," I heard Alex speak. "Thank you for showing us the house. I'll be in touch."

"I have a couple who is highly interested in it, so if I were you, I wouldn't wait too long to make a decision."

We climbed in the car and a feeling of peace flowed through me.

"Thank you, Parker."

He grabbed my hand and brought it up to his lips. "You're welcome. We better get home and change out of these wet clothes."

Chapter 31

Emerson

Seeing my childhood home brought back so many memories. Memories of the happiness that once resided there. After changing out of my wet clothes, Alex knocked on my bedroom door.

"Come in."

He walked in and over to me as I was putting on my shirt.

"Emerson," he spoke.

"What's up, Parker?" I smiled.

"We need to talk," he spoke with a serious tone.

"Okay. Shoot, big guy."

He took hold of both my hands. Staring into my eyes, he inhaled deeply.

"Em, I—" He paused.

"What is it, Alex? Is something wrong?"

He gave me a small smile. "No. I just wanted to tell you that I'm happy I took you to the house."

"Thank you. I'm happy that you did too. I'm sorry I gave you shit about it when we first got there and, again, I'm sorry for threatening your balls."

He laughed. "Apology accepted." He kissed my forehead. "I'm going to head to the office. I'll be home later tonight."

"Okay."

He walked out and I stared at the door. I was hoping he'd come to tell me something else. But he didn't. I was so scared of what was happening because things were changing for me. Feelings for Alex were stronger than ever. Was this real? Could this be real? I should tell him how I feel. But then if the feelings weren't returned, I would be left standing like a fool. Alex Parker didn't do relationships because of frizzy, curly-haired girl. I didn't do relationships because the thought of attaching myself to someone and then losing them scared the living hell out of me. Never stay in one place long enough to become attached.

****

Alex

As I was sitting in my office, I stared out the window and thought of Emerson. I should have told her how I felt. I should have told her that I loved her right then and there, like I had planned to. But when I looked into her eyes, I couldn't. She was strong and she was determined and she was going to leave. What if she didn't love me back? I thought maybe she did, but I wasn't sure. For the first time in my life, I was scared. Scared of being rejected by the first woman I had ever truly loved. Was I just another broken heart in her eyes? Another guy she'd leave behind while she traveled off on her next adventure? This was killing me. She was killing me. I spent the night at the office.

The next morning, when I returned home to change and shower, I found Emerson in the kitchen.

"Hey. You didn't come home last night," she spoke.

"I had so much work to do and I fell asleep."

"Oh. I hope you slept okay. I sent you a couple of text messages but you didn't reply."

I shrugged. "I'm just home to shower and change."

She looked down and I looked away.

"Okay. I hope your day goes better."

"Thanks." I went upstairs and sat on the edge of my bed, placing my face in my hands for a moment before showering and leaving again.

After spending the day thinking about Emerson and looking up the definition of love once again, I had no choice but to tell her how much I loved her. I wasn't letting her go anywhere. She belonged here with me. We belonged together whether she believed it or not. I had stopped by the florist and picked up a dozen red roses for her. I was going to make her see that staying in California was the best thing for her. That I was the best thing for her.

When I arrived home, I couldn't find her.

"Jenna, where's Emerson?"

She looked at me and then looked down.

"Jenna?"

"She's gone, Mr. Parker."

"WHAT?! What do you mean 'she's gone'?" I said through gritted teeth in an angry tone that I believe scared the poor woman.

"She packed her bags and left."

"Did she say where she was going?"

"No. She just said she had to leave."

"FUCK!" I screamed and she flinched.

I stormed out of the kitchen and down the hall to Emerson's room. Flinging open the door, I walked inside and looked around. The closet was empty, as were all her drawers. Lying on the bed was a sealed envelope with my name on it. I picked it up and sat down. Pulling out the letter, I unfolded it and a picture of the two of us fell to the ground. Picking it up and looking at it for a moment, I held it in my hand as I began to read the words she wrote.

My dearest Alex,

Two words come to mind as I'm sitting here writing this. Thank you. Thank you for everything you've done for me. Never stay in one place too long, right? Spending the past months with you have been the most amazing time I'd ever had. I know you probably aren't believing that, but they were. I was scared to come back, yet you managed to turn my fears into ashes. When I was with you, I didn't think about anything else. You made me feel safe and secure and you gave your home to me. For that, I thank you. I told you things I had never told anyone because you made me feel comfortable and protected. I hadn't felt that way in a very long time. You made me fall in love with you, Parker. Something no one has ever been able to do. You took care of me even when you didn't realize it. You gave me hope for the future. Something I hadn't had since the accident. There's so much beauty in this world, even underneath all the despair and tragedies. I see that because of you. When you took me home, you gave me memories I didn't think I had and I can't even begin to thank you enough for that. I hope you can understand why I had to leave and why I couldn't face you in person. Hell, I'm not sure I even understand, so if you don't, it's okay. You've forgiven me for things I've said and I hope you can forgive me for leaving. You're not just another guy I left behind. You're the man who stole my heart. I had the picture printed so you could have it and always remember me. I hope you don't mind. If you don't want it, throw it out. I wouldn't blame you if you did. You're my best friend, Alex Parker, and I love you. Make sure to take your medication every day and stay away from the saltshaker. Actually, that won't be difficult at home because I threw them all out. But I trust that when you're out and you see a saltshaker, you won't touch it because you'll hear my voice in your head. I'm looking out for you like you did me. Take care, Parker, and promise me you'll never forget me.

Love forever,

Emerson

The air in the room became thick and it was difficult to breathe. She did love me and if I had only confessed my feelings for her, she might have stayed. I crumpled up the letter in my hand and tossed it on the bed. As I looked at the picture of the two of us in Napa, tears started to form in my eyes. I already missed her, and suddenly, my world fell apart.

As I wiped the tears from my eyes, my phone rang. It was Adam. Shit.

"Hello."

"She's gone again. Isn't she?"

"Yes."

"Damn it. I thought you were going to convince her to stay." He sounded angry.

"I tried. Do you know where she would have gone?"

"How the fuck would I know? I never knew where she was until she called and told me."

"How did you know she was gone?"

"She left a letter on my door. Apologizing and asking for forgiveness. But the thing is, I don't think I can forgive her this time."

"You can, Adam."

"Can you, Alex?"

"Yes, because I love her."

"If you hear from her, call me. I tried texting her, but my texts won't go through."

"I will."

I ended the call and lay back on the bed, staring at the picture of us.

Chapter 32

Alex

I was still lying on Emerson's bed when Jenna knocked on the door and slowly opened it.

"Excuse me, Mr. Parker."

"What?!" I spoke in a stern voice.

"Umm. You need to come to the front door. A package arrived for you."

"Just bring it here."

"Are you sure?"

"Jenna, bring the goddamn package to me!" I yelled.

"Very well."

A few moments later, she walked back in the bedroom and a look of shock splayed across my face.

"What the hell is that?" I asked as she held a puppy in her arms.

"This was the package at the front door."

She set him down on the bed and he began to jump on me and lick my face.

"Oh my God. Get it out of here!"

She picked up the dog and handed me an envelope. "This was with it, sir."

I took it from her hand and opened it, pulling out the white card inside.

"Alex,

I want you to meet Parker. In case you can't tell, he's a yellow Lab and he's just a baby. Take good care of him for me. You need him as much as he needs you. Take him to the beach and play fetch with him. Teach him some tricks and talk to him. You need someone to love, Alex, and he won't break your heart.

Love always,

Emerson."

What the hell was she thinking? I looked up at Jenna, who was standing there petting the puppy.

"It's from Emerson and his name is Parker."

She laughed and I shot her a look.

"I guess we have a new houseguest, Jenna. You may place him on the bed."

She set him down and, instantly, he ran over to me, licking my face and jumping all around. I took hold of his red collar with the dog-bone-shaped tag attached to it that read: *Parker Parker*. I couldn't help but laugh because this was so Emerson.

****

I spent the next couple of weeks working from home and bonding with Parker. He was a cute little guy and I wasn't even fond of dogs, especially when they shit in the house. We spent a lot of time on the beach and playing in the yard.

I missed Emerson so much and, every day that passed, it hurt more and more. I hadn't shaven in a few days and I didn't care. A feeling of hopelessness resided in me without her in my life. All I wanted was to hear her sweet voice and hold her in my arms once again. She changed me, my life, and my world. And my world was nothing without her in it.

"Excuse me, Mr. Parker," Jenna spoke as she stepped out onto the patio.

"Yes, Jenna?"

"Emerson left something behind."

"What?"

"This." She held out the map Emerson always kept with her.

Staring at it for a moment, my heart started racing. I looked at Jenna.

"She wouldn't have left this behind. This would have been the first thing she packed. Where did you find it?"

"I was in her room dusting and Parker dragged it out from under the bed."

Suddenly, a feeling of happiness flowed inside me.

"Jenna, do you know what this means?" I smiled as I took the map from her.

"No, sir. I don't."

"Emerson left this behind because she wants me to find her! Come inside."

I unfolded the map and laid it on the island. "The black circles are the places she still had to go. The red circles are the places she's already been. Focus on the black circles, Jenna."

We both stared intently at the map.

"She could be anywhere," Jenna spoke.

My eyes diverted to the right side of the map. "I know where she's at!" I exclaimed.

"Where? How do you know?"

"She's right here." I smiled as I pointed to the state of Maine. "Bass Harbor holds a special place in her memories and I know that's where she went!"

Without even thinking, I grabbed Jenna and kissed her forehead.

"Sir?" she said in a shocked tone.

"I need you to stay here for a few days and watch Parker for me. I'll pay you double what you're making now. I'm going to bring Emerson home, Jenna." I smiled. "I'm bringing her back and she's never leaving again unless I'm with her."

"Go, sir. I'll stay with Parker. Go get her!" She smiled.

I pulled out my phone and dialed my pilot.

"Hello, Mr. Parker."

"Get the plane ready. We're going to Bass Harbor, Maine."

"When would you like to leave?"

"I'll be there in an hour. I don't have any time to waste."

"Very well, sir. I'll be waiting for you."

I ended the call and dialed Phillip.

"Phillip. I need you to come get me and take me to my plane. I know where Emerson is and I'm going to bring her home."

"Excellent news, Alex. I'll be there in about ten minutes."

Chapter 33

Emerson

I rented a cottage on the water in Bass Harbor, Maine. When I first arrived, I didn't have a plan and I was lucky that Pine Cottages had one left to rent. It was small but quaint. It had a living area with a fireplace, which I was grateful for since the weather in Maine was getting quite chilly, a small bedroom with a queen-size bed, and a small kitchen area with a stove, sink, and refrigerator.

I spent my days walking along the rocky shores and watching the lobster boats drift by. I spent my nights missing Alex so much that it hurt. There wasn't one second of the day where I wasn't thinking about him.

"Hello, Emerson." Mary knocked on the door.

"Come on in, Mary."

She opened the door and handed me a fresh loaf of bread she had just made. Mary was the owner of Pine Cottages and we had quickly become friends. Her husband had passed away a few years ago and she never had any children. The cottages were everything to her. Sometimes at night, she would come over and we'd sit out on the screened-in porch, talking about life and drinking tea. I told her everything; the accident, my travels, and all about Alex.

"He still hasn't shown up, eh?"

"No. But he will. If he knows me at all, he'll find me."

"So that's what you're waiting on? Him to find you to see if he's the one to change your life and get you to settle?"

"Yep. I confessed my feelings to him in that letter and if he feels the same about me, he'll come."

"I still don't understand why you didn't tell him how you felt back in California."

I gave her a small smile. "It's complicated. He's complicated. I'm complicated. But together, we're uncomplicated. Does that make sense?"

She laughed. "Not really. But I'll take your word for it." She reached over and patted my hand. "I was thinking that maybe tomorrow morning you can help me in the kitchen. Maybe show me a thing or two you learned in Tuscany."

"I'd love to."

"Great. Then I'll see you up at the main house around seven a.m.?"

"I will be there."

****

Alex

Due to a slight mechanical problem, I couldn't take off as planned and I was angry. The only thing I wanted to do was get to Emerson. But then I was faced with another problem. I didn't know where the hell she was staying, so I called Adam.

"Hello."

"Adam, I know where Emerson's at."

"Did you hear from her?"

"No. But she left her map behind."

"Huh? That's unlike her."

"Exactly. She wants me to find her."

"Where is she?"

"Bass Harbor, Maine."

"How do you know she's there?"

"When I took her back to your childhood home, she told me the story about your parents and the lighthouses. She hasn't been to Maine yet. It was still circled in black."

"I remember that story. Do you really think she's there?"

"Yes. I do. I'm almost sure of it. I need you to look at her credit card to see what hotel she checked into."

"Sorry, Alex. I don't have access to that anymore."

"Shit. Okay. I'll figure it out. If I have to search every hotel in Bass Harbor and the surrounding area, I will."

"Good luck. Bring her home, Alex."

"I will. I'll talk to you soon."

I pulled up Google on my phone and searched Bass Harbor, Maine. The first thing that popped up was cottage rentals. My mind flashed back to when we were at her house. She told me that her parents rented a cottage on the water during their stay. Those cottages would be the first place I'd look.

Finally, the mechanical issue was fixed and the plane was able to take off. Since it was an eight-hour flight, I wouldn't be getting into the Bangor Airport until three a.m. I sighed. Now I'd have to find a hotel since I couldn't go around trying to find her in the middle of the night. Damn it, of all places not to have a hotel chain. I was going to have to do something about that. I dialed Simon.

"Hey, Alex. What can I do for you?"

"Hey, Simon. Do you by any chance have a hotel in Bangor, Maine?"

"Maine? No. I don't."

"Shit. You know, we really need to talk about opening one up there."

"Why? What's in Maine?"

"I'm going to find Emerson and I need a hotel to stay at for the night. I won't be getting in until three a.m."

"Ah. I see. What part of Maine?"

"I'm flying into Bangor."

"That's a really small airport. I'm not sure what hotels are around there."

"I'll find something. Thanks, Simon. I'll talk to you soon."

"Sorry I couldn't help. Talk to you soon."

I sighed as I pulled up a list of hotels in Bangor. I stumbled across a Marriott. It would have to do. I booked my room and sat back, pulling up the video of us singing in the car on our way back from Napa.

****

It was nine o'clock in the morning when I hopped into the rental car I rented and headed to Bass Harbor. If I had realized that it was an hour and a half drive, I would have left earlier. Failed planning on my part. I followed the GPS and arrived at the first set of cottages in Bass Harbor around ten thirty. She wasn't staying at any of those. Shit. The people there told me there was another set of cottages up about ten miles near the lighthouse. Pulling up to Pine Cottages, I saw a woman walking out of the main house. I parked the car and got out. She stood there looking at me.

"I'm sorry, but we don't have any more cottages to rent."

"I'm looking for someone. I'm hoping you could help me out."

She stood there, her eyes glaring at me as I approached her. The corners of her mouth curved upwards.

"Well, I'll be damned. It's nice to finally meet you, Alex Parker." She held out her hand.

I tilted my head and narrowed my eye at her as I lightly shook her hand. "She's here. Isn't she?"

"Yes, and she's been waiting for you. I'm Mary. I own this place. Come with me. I'll take you to her cottage."

I followed her down a short path. "She told you about me?" I asked.

"Oh yes. She even showed me your picture. That's how I knew who you were. Emerson and I became friends quite quickly."

"I'm not surprised." I smiled.

"I just saw her this morning. She was helping in my kitchen. Teaching me a few things she learned in Tuscany."

"She's a wonderful cook."

"She sure is. She made a pot of lobster stew the other night that practically knocked my socks off."

When we approached a small white cottage, Mary knocked on the door.

"Emerson, it's Mary. Open up, sweetie."

No answer. She knocked again.

"She mustn't be here." She reached into her pocket and pulled out a ring of keys. Inserting it into the lock, she opened the door and we stepped inside.

"You can wait for her here if you want. Set your bags down and relax until she gets back."

"Thank you, Mary. I have a place I'm going to check out first. Maybe she's there."

"The lighthouse?" She gave me a smile.

"You know the story?" I asked.

"I sure do. It's about a ten-minute walk from here. Go up the path and follow it until you reach the rocks. The lighthouse is on the other side. She spends a lot of time there. She's probably there now."

"I hope so. Thank you again for your help. I appreciate it."

"No problem. Good luck, Alex. It was nice to finally meet you."

I gave her a nod and followed the path like she said. When I reached the rocks, I could see Emerson sitting in front of the lighthouse. My heart started racing. I'd found her.

Chapter 34

Emerson

As I was sitting on the rocks, looking out into the ocean, a light wind swept across my face. I would never grow tired of the beauty of this place. Holding my phone in my hand, I pulled up the video I took of us. My heart ached as I watched it for the hundredth time. God, did I miss him and his man scent. I set my phone down and placed my face in my hands.

"It's time to come home, Emerson."

I lifted my head and froze for a moment as my heart started to rapidly beat and my stomach started to flutter. I slowly turned around and smiled when I saw Alex standing up on the rocks. Tears started to fill my eyes as I stood up.

"Stay there. I'll come to you." He smiled as he made his way down the rocks.

When he reached me, I threw my arms around him and buried my face into the side of his neck.

"You knew where to find me."

"Of course I did. Give me those damn lips." He commanded.

I lifted my head and our lips met, engaging in a passionate kiss that I never wanted to end.

"How's Parker? You have Parker, right? I mean, you didn't give him away or kick his little puppy ass to the street, did you?"

Alex chuckled. "Parker is fine. We bonded. Now why are we talking about the dog? We haven't seen each other in weeks and you want to talk about the dog?"

I laughed as I planted many kisses all over his face.

"I missed you so much, Alex."

"I missed you too, baby."

"Did you just call me 'baby'?" I smiled.

"I did and I'm going to keep calling you that whether you like it or not."

He placed his hands on each side of my face. "I love you, Emerson James. I'm madly in love with you and you're never leaving me again. Do you understand me?"

"Yes." I nodded. "I totally understand and I'm not even mad that you took that commanding tone with me." I smiled.

He smiled as he placed his forehead on mine. "I love you so much and I'm never letting you go. I want you back home with me. It's our home, Emerson. Mine and yours. California doesn't have to be that place of tragic memories for you anymore."

"I know and I want to come home. I missed you so much."

His smile widened as his lips touched mine. "That's what I wanted to hear." He pulled me into a tight embrace.

We sat down on the rocks in front of the lighthouse, our arms wrapped tightly around each other, staring out into the ocean.

"It truly is beautiful here," he spoke.

"It sure is." I kissed his cheek.

"I met Mary. She seems like a really nice lady."

"She is. She's amazing. How did you know where I was staying?"

"I remember you saying that your parents stayed in a cottage while they were here."

"So you were really listening to me."

He looked over at me and pushed a strand of hair behind my ear. "I always listen to every word you say, Emerson, and I promise you that I will never stop. These past weeks have been fucking torture for me. I wasn't able to concentrate on anything. Parker and I had a long conversation about you and he can't wait until you come home. But I'm afraid he's taken over your side of the bed."

I laughed. "Have you been sleeping in my bed?"

"Some nights I did because I felt closer to you. But that's not your bed anymore. You will be in our bed upstairs."

I raised my eyebrow at him. "I've never been in your bed. What if I don't like it?"

"Trust me." He smiled. "You're going to love it. I'm sorry I never brought you up there."

"Nah. It's okay. We were comfortable in my room. Speaking of which, I think we need to head back to the cottage. We have some serious sex to make up."

"You read my mind, Emerson. I can't wait to explore that perfect body of yours again."

Our lips locked one last time before getting up and heading back to the cottage.

****

A trail of clothes lined the floor from the door to the bed. To be touched by Alex again was a dream. I'd missed his hands caressing my body and I'd missed his tongue exploring every inch of my bare skin.

"God, you feel so good, baby," he moaned as he moved in and out of me.

Our bodies were covered in sweat from the amazing foreplay we had. The type of foreplay where Alex gave me two over-the-top orgasms. His thrusting became faster as his lips wrapped around my nipple and my legs tightened around his waist. His mouth met mine as he nipped my bottom lip. Throwing my head back, several loud moans escaped me.

"That's it, baby. Come for me. Show me how much you love me inside of you."

"Alex," I spoke loudly as my body shook from another amazing orgasm.

"Fuck, Em," he moaned as he pushed deeper and spilled his come inside me.

After holding each other for few moments, he rolled off of me and we both lay on our sides, facing each other as he ran his finger along my jaw.

"I love you," he spoke in a soft tone.

"I love you, too, Alex. I wanted to tell you so badly but I was scared."

"Scared of what, baby?"

"Scared of loving you because if something happened to you, I wouldn't be able to handle it."

He leaned over and kissed me. "Nothing's going to happen to me. I'm always going to be with you."

"Have you been taking your medication?"

He frowned. "Of course."

"Have you been watching your salt intake?"

"Yes. I have, Miss Bossy Pants." He smiled. "And I can't believe you threw away the salt shakers."

"I couldn't take the chance."

"I could have just gone to the store and bought more."

"You wouldn't have. You won't go the store unless I drag you there."

"True." He kissed me again. "How about we get dressed, grab something to eat, and you can show me around Bass Harbor."

"Sounds good, but first, I need just one more orgasm."

He smirked. "You're awful greedy, Miss James." His hand brushed over my bare breast.

"It's your fault, Mr. Parker. If you didn't make me feel so good all the time, my body wouldn't be craving you so much."

His hand traveled from my breast, down my torso, and cupped me down below.

“Are you sure you only want one more?”

“For now, yes. But tonight, you better prepare yourself to make me come at least three more times.”

“It would be my pleasure.” He plunged a finger inside me and smashed his mouth against mine.

Chapter 35

Alex

"Wake up, sleepy head!"

Opening my eyes, I saw Emerson standing over me with a cup of coffee.

"What time is it?" I yawned.

"Six o'clock."

"Six? Why are you up handing me coffee at six o'clock in the morning? We're on vacation."

"Because we have to be at the lobster boat at seven." She smiled.

"Lobster boat? What are you talking about?" I sat up and took the coffee from her.

"We're going to haul some traps out of the water." She grinned. "It's fun, and Rick and Devon will be waiting for us at seven. So come on, Parker. Get up and get dressed."

I sighed. "Come here and give me a kiss first before we have a discussion."

She rolled her eyes at me before leaning over and kissing me.

"First of all, Emerson, who are Rick and Devon?"

"They're the lobster fishermen and my friends."

"You haven't been here that long. How many friends have you made?"

She shrugged. "I don't know. A few. Rick and Devon supply Mary with the lobsters. I was talking to Mary one day and they just brought in a shipment. I was curious, so they told me they'd show me how it's done."

"So while I was at home, pissing and moaning and missing the hell out of you, you were here trapping lobsters?"

"I never once stopped thinking about you. I had to keep busy while I was waiting for you to come or I would have gone crazy."

"Okay, fair enough. Now, you can't call me Parker anymore. That's the dog's name and if you call me that in front of him, he'll get all confused."

"Can I still call you Parker when he's not around?" She grinned.

I set my coffee cup on the nightstand, grabbed her, and pinned her down on the bed.

"No. You cannot!" I smiled as I kissed her.

"Fine. Come on. Make sure you dress warm. It's cold on that boat."

"How cold? I didn't pack anything warm. I didn't expect it to be cold here."

"Hmm. Okay, hurry up and throw some clothes on that sexy body. There's a shop up the road that sells clothes. We'll find you something there."

"I'm sure they're not open this early."

"They open at five a.m."

"Can I shower first?"

"I wouldn't. You'll get pretty stinky on that boat. Wait until we come back."

"Great. Are you sure you want to do this?" I asked.

"Yes. You don't?"

As I stared into her beautiful blue eyes, I saw nothing but excitement in them.

"Of course I do. I want to do anything you want to. It'll be quite the experience. I've never been on a lobster boat before."

I kissed her one last time, went into the bathroom, brushed my teeth, and threw on some clothes. When I walked out of the bedroom, Emerson gave me a weird look.

"What? What's wrong?"

"Don't you have a pair of jeans?" she asked.

I looked down at my khakis. "No. Have you ever seen me in jeans?"

"No. But I think you should wear them."

"I don't like jeans." I walked over to the pot and poured another cup of coffee.

"Why?"

"I don't know." She looked adorable in her jeans and zip-up hoodie.

"Come on, big guy, let's go buy you something warm." She took hold of my hand and we walked to the store up the road.

"Hey, Emerson," a man yelled from behind the counter.

"Hi, Rob." She smiled at him.

"Another friend?" I asked.

"Yep. He and his wife own the store. We got to talking one day when I was in here looking around."

She pulled out a black zip-up hoodie from the rack and held it up to me. "Do you like this?"

"It's okay. I prefer gray."

"Here's gray." She smiled. "Try it on."

As I was trying it on, she walked over to the wall where the jeans were folded neatly on the shelf. There was no way I was putting on a pair of jeans.

"Emerson," I yelled as I held out my hands. "How does it look?"

"I like it!" Her grin widened. "But not with those pants. Come over here and pick out your size in a pair of jeans."

I sighed as I walked over to where she was standing. "I don't want a pair of jeans, sweetheart."

She looked at me, tilted her head, and placed her hand firmly on my chest. "It's time to step out of the corporate big boy clothes and into something comfy. Just try them on and humor me. Please," she whined.

I glared at her. "Fine. I'll try them on."

I went into the fitting room and tried on the jeans. When I walked out, Emerson whistled.

"Look at you." She bit down on her bottom lip. "Turn around so I can see that hot ass."

I rolled my eyes and turned around. She walked up behind me and grabbed me.

"Perfect. Just perfect." She kissed my cheek. "But you're missing one thing."

"What?"

"Hold on. I'll be right back."

A few moments later, she returned with a knit hat and put it over my head.

"There. Fuck, Alex. You are hot in that outfit. Turn around and look at yourself in the mirror."

"Are you saying that I don't look hot in my other clothes, Emerson?"

"No. You're hot all the time. But right now, I think my ovaries just exploded."

I laughed. "What?"

"Forget it. I'm not explaining it to you." She reached up and whispered in my ear, "You have no idea the things I want to do to you right now while you're wearing those clothes. Bad things. Very bad things, Alex."

My cock was getting hard. "Emerson, stop. For the love of God, don't say another word. Fine, I'll buy these."

"Only buy them if you're comfortable in them."

"I'm comfortable, Emerson."

"Are you sure?"

I grabbed her hips and faced her. "I'm comfortable. Now be quiet." I softly kissed her lips.

"Good." She ripped the tags off the clothes and took them up to the register.

Chapter 36

Emerson

We spent a few hours on the lobster boat and Alex helped haul the traps. He was so sexy and it was good to see him enjoying himself. At least I think he was. I made him hold up a large lobster while I took his picture and sent it to Jenna.

"Look at Alex!"

"OMG! He looks like a normal person, LOL!"

"I know, right? Doesn't he look sexy in that knit hat? And look, he's wearing jeans."

"He is hot. Don't tell him I said that."

"LOL. I won't."

I handed my phone to Rick. "Can you take a picture of me and Alex holding the lobster?"

"Sure thing, Emerson." He smiled.

I stood next to Alex and kissed his cheek while holding on to one of the lobster's claws. Once the boat took us back to the dock, we thanked Rick and Devon and began walking back to the cottage.

"That was really cool." Alex smiled as he kissed my head.

"I'm glad you enjoyed yourself."

"That was something I never thought I would like doing."

"See how fun life can be when you step out of your corporate world?"

"Yes, and speaking of which, we need to head back tomorrow."

"I figured as much. I've spent enough time here anyway." I laid my head on his shoulder.

When we got back to the cottage, Alex turned on the fireplace. "Come here," he said.

Walking over to him, I fell right into his arms. "I love you."

"I love you too." My lips touched his.

His fingers unzipped my hoodie and he slid it off my shoulders. Unzipping his, I tossed it on the floor and lifted his shirt over his head. He went to take the hat off and I stopped him.

"Leave it on." I smiled.

"Really?" He arched his brow.

"Yes. Really. I find it incredibly sexy."

He laughed as he lifted off my t-shirt. "Fine. But I don't want you wearing a damn thing when I fuck you."

He reached back and unhooked my bra, letting the straps fall down. Groping my breasts with his strong hands, I reached for the button on his jeans as he did mine. Kicking them off, we tossed them to the side and Alex laid me down on the floor in front of the warm fire.

"Are you warm?" he asked as his tongue slid down over my breasts.

"Very." I smiled as my fingers tangled in his hair.

Hooking his fingers into the side of my panties, he pulled them down and slid his tongue along my soaking wet opening, forcing me to have an orgasm. My body shook in delight as he grabbed hold of my hands and held them over my head.

"I enjoyed that." He grinned.

"Me too." I smiled as I stared into his beautiful brown eyes.

He rolled on his back and pulled me on top of him. "Ride me, baby."

I moaned as I smashed my mouth into his and felt his hard cock at my opening. He thrust inside me and I gasped. Sitting up, I took him all the way in and slowly moved back and forth, circling my hips a few times and watching the expression of pleasure on his face. His hands groped my breasts and his fingers played with my hardened nipples. His low moans were getting louder, as were mine the faster I moved. His hips thrust up and he moved in and out of me at a rapid pace, causing me to ride the wave of another amazing orgasm.

"Fuck, baby. Go. Don't stop. I'm so close," he whimpered.

Riding him faster, his grip on my hips tightened as he strained and poured himself inside me.

My heart was racing at the speed of light and my breathing was rapid. He pulled me down on top of him, holding me tight while I buried my face into his neck. We lay there for a few moments in silence, trying to regain our normal breathing rate.

I lifted my head and kissed his lips. He smiled as he pushed my hair from my face. "You are amazing."

"So are you. Not to ruin this beautiful moment, but I'm starving."

He chuckled. "Me too."

I climbed off of him and we went into the bathroom and took a shower together. The tub was really small, and it was difficult, but nonetheless, we made it work.

After having lunch, we did some shopping. We stumbled upon a small art gallery not too far from the cottage. Hanging on the wall was a portrait of the Bass Harbor Lighthouse.

"Is this the same painting your parents had?" Alex asked.

"No. It's different. It's so beautiful." I ran my finger along it.

Alex called the sales lady over and told her he would like to purchase the painting.

"Really?" I asked excitedly.

"Of course, Emerson. We're going to hang this in our house as a memory of the start of our future together as a couple."

My heart melted when I heard him speak those words. I wrapped my arms around him and laid my head on his chest.

"Thank you, Alex. And you said you weren't a romantic guy."

"To be honest, I never was until you walked into my life."

****

Alex

We were sitting on the plane, sprawled out on the couch with Emerson's head on my lap. She was finally coming home where she belonged. There wasn't anything I wouldn't do for her. I loved her so much and I never wanted to be apart from her again.

"Emerson, there's something I have to say."

"What is it?" she asked as she looked up at me.

"Just because you're coming home doesn't mean you have to stop seeing the places on your map. I promise you that we're going to go to all the places you have left. You're never going to have to go alone again. I want to see everything you and Emily talked about. I want to explore the world with you."

She gave me a small smile as she reached up and placed her hand on my cheek. "Thank you. That means so much to me, but if you noticed, the map is almost full of red circles."

"Then how about we start our own map?"

"Really? Do you really mean that?" she asked in excitement.

"Yes. I really mean it. I would do anything for you."

****

We were finally back in California and Phillip was waiting for us with the Bentley.

"Welcome back, Emerson. I hope you're here to stay."

"I am, Phillip, and thank you. It's good to be home."

Opening the door to the house, Parker came running to us.

"Oh my God! There's my baby," Emerson screeched as she bent down and Parker licked her face.

"Welcome home, Mr. Parker and Emerson." Jenna smiled.

"You can call him Alex. You'll confuse the dog if you call him Parker. Right?" She looked over at me.

"Right." I slowly nodded my head. "You may call me Alex, Jenna."

"Oh. Okay," she spoke with a hint of fear in her voice.

I grabbed both of our bags and headed up the stairs, Emerson following behind. When we reached my bedroom, she stopped in the doorway.

"What are you doing?" I asked.

"Making sure it's okay to step inside His Majesty's quarters."

I took in a deep breath and glared at her for a moment. With a smile on my face, I walked over to her, picked her up, and carried her inside the room.

"This is our quarters now, Your Highness." I softly kissed her lips before setting her on the bed.

Parker ran into the bedroom and jumped on the bed, jumping all over Emerson.

"Do you like this bed, Parker?" she asked as she grabbed his face.

I stood there watching her play with the dog, and my heart melted. I knew she'd make a wonderful mother someday.

"There's something I need to do," she spoke with seriousness.

"Adam?" I asked.

"Yeah."

Walking over to the bed, I sat down next to her and Parker went wild all over me.

"Why don't we have him over tomorrow for dinner and the two of you can talk." I grabbed hold of him and pinned him down, rubbing his belly.

"I think it's best if I talk to him at his house. Come here, my little baby."

I leaned over to kiss her.

"Not you. The dog!" She smiled as she got up from the bed.

"I don't think I'm going to like sharing your attention with the dog," I spoke.

"I have plenty of attention to go around," she spoke as she grabbed my face and kissed me.

Chapter 37

Emerson

The next morning, as I was cooking breakfast, my phone rang and it was Adam.

"Hey," I answered.

"Hey. I saw you called last night. I was out and, by time I got home, it was too late to call you. Where are you?"

"At Alex's house."

"I see."

"Adam, we need to talk. I need to talk to you."

"I'm going to the cemetery at eleven o'clock. If you want to talk, that's where I'll be."

The tone of his voice was flat. He was still hurt and mad at me and it killed me inside that I did that to my brother.

I took in a deep breath. "I'll meet you there."

"When you turn into the cemetery, take a left on the first turn. Go down about a quarter mile and their graves are on the left."

"Okay. I'll see you soon."

Just as I set my phone down, Alex walked in with Parker.

"Did he go?"

"Yep. He sure did." He walked over and kissed me. "What's wrong? You seem upset?"

"Adam just called. I'm meeting him at the cemetery at eleven to talk."

Alex sighed and wrapped his arms around me, pulling me into him. "Do you want me to go with you?"

"Thanks for the offer, but I'll be okay. This is something I need to do on my own."

"Okay. But if you need me, I can be there in a flash."

I broke our embrace and kissed his lips. "I'll be okay."

"I know you'll be." He softly smiled. "Is breakfast ready? I'm starving."

"Yes. Breakfast is ready. Go sit down."

"Have I told you how much I love you?"

"Nah. You only love me for my mad cooking skills."

"Maybe, but I also love you for your mad fucking skills." He smirked.

"Get your ass to the table, you dirty-talking man." I slapped his ass with the spatula.

"Make sure you bring that to bed tonight." He pointed at me with a grin on his face.

****

The pit of my stomach was twisted in knots as I pulled into the cemetery. Making a left on the first turn, I saw Adam's car parked at the curb. I pulled behind him and took in a long, deep breath as I got out of the car. Feeling sick to my stomach, I leaned against the car for a moment to collect myself. I could see Adam straight ahead, kneeling on the ground. Slowly walking over to him, I stared at the headstones that displayed my sister's and parents' names.

"Hey," I spoke as I placed my hand on my brother's shoulder.

He turned and looked at me, squinting his eyes as the warm sun beat down on us.

"Hey. Thanks for coming."

I knelt down beside him. "The headstones are beautiful."

"Yeah, they are. When did you get back?" he asked without looking at me.

"Yesterday."

"Are you staying?"

"Yeah. I'm staying."

"So you and Alex are a thing now?"

"Yes. We're dating and living together. Is that okay?"

He glanced over at me. "Are you happy?"

"Yeah. I love him, Adam."

"Then it's okay." He reached over, grabbed my hand, and gave me a small smile.

"Listen, I'm so sorry for everything. You're my brother and all the family I have left and I really screwed us up over the past eight years."

"I understand now why you left, Em. But I was here to help you get through it."

I looked down at the ground and pulled a weed. "I didn't want help, Adam. I just wanted to escape the reality of what happened. It was a nightmare that I couldn't wake up from and the only sense of peace I could find was to try and live the dream Emily and I had. You were right all along; I was running. Running away from the accident, the deaths, and my home. But I'm home now and this is where I'm staying."

He hooked his arm around me and pulled me into him. Laying my head on his shoulder, I smiled.

"I'm happy you're back, sis. I want our relationship back."

"I will spend the next eight years making it up to you."

"Only eight?" He laughed.

"Yeah. I was only gone for eight, so why would I take any more time than that?"

He sighed. "Sometimes I wonder how Alex puts up with you and that mouth."

"Between me and you, he loves it when I give him attitude. It turns him on."

"Okay. That's enough. I don't need to be hearing things like that about my friend and my sister."

I laughed as I lifted my head and looked at him. Kissing his cheek, I spoke, "Thank you."

"For what?"

"For making me come back and stay with Alex. If it wasn't for you, we never would have met and I wouldn't have fallen in love with him."

"You're welcome. It's still strange to me, though. Of all people, Alex Parker was the one I wasn't worried about. In fact, the only thing that worried me was that he'd kick you out on your ass before I got back."

"Thanks!" I laughed.

He shrugged. "It's the truth."

"It's pretty here. Have you been keeping the grave sites up?"

"Yep. I come every Sunday and tend to things."

I looked at the headstones once again and then got up and ran my finger along them.

"They're always with us, you know," I spoke.

"Yeah. I know. That night after our argument, I came home, opened a beer, and sat down on the couch. When I turned the TV on, it shut off and the picture I had on the wall behind the couch fell down. Scared the shit out of me. When I got up and picked it up, the room suddenly got really cold. I threw my hands up and said I was sorry for being such an asshole. The TV turned on by itself after that. I knew it was Emily or the parents yelling at me for the way I talked to you."

"Probably." I walked over to him as he stood up and wrapped my arms around him. Suddenly, I felt raindrops hit my skin.

"They weren't calling for rain today," Adam spoke as he broke our embrace and held his hands up.

"No, they weren't. But it can rain all it wants." I smiled.

Chapter 38

Emerson

Six Weeks Later

Life was wonderful. Alex and I were wonderful. In fact, we were perfect. Was that possible? Yes. With me and Alex, it was. I was out and about running some errands and thinking about him, missing him, and craving his kisses. Looking at my watch, I decided to pick up lunch, bring it to his office, and surprise him. After picking up some salads, I headed to his building. As the elevator doors opened, I stepped out and headed to his office. Apparently, his secretary, Olivia, must have been at lunch because she wasn't at her desk. When I reached his office, I noticed the door was slightly open. As I was about ready to lightly knock, I saw him through the crack of the open door. My eyes widened and my stomach fell sick with what I saw. He was locked in an embrace with Bella. The two of them, alone in his office, hugging, and not a quick hug, but a long embrace. My heart started pounding out of my chest and it was hard to breathe. I went to the stairwell and, like a mad woman, flew down thirty flights of stairs. Making it to the lobby, I ran out the front doors of the building and down the street to where I had parked my car. Once I was inside, uncontrollable tears streamed down my face. When I finally calmed down as much as I could, I drove home. My mind was a train wreck and I needed to get a grip on myself.

When I arrived home, Jenna was in the kitchen. She could tell something was wrong the minute she turned and looked at me.

"Are you okay? What happened?"

Did I tell her? We had become very close since I moved back and she trusted me with things that she had never told anyone before. I needed to talk to someone, so I took a seat at the island.

"I went to Alex's office to bring him lunch and I found him in there in a tight embrace with Bella."

"WHAT?!" she exclaimed.

I wiped my eyes as the tears started to fall again.

"Did he see you?"

I shook my head. "No. The door was only open a crack."

"Emerson." She took hold of my hands. "There's a perfectly reasonable explanation. There has to be. Alex would never do that to you. He loves you so much. I have never seen him so happy."

"I don't know anymore."

Parker was whining at me.

"Okay, stop right there. You're jumping to conclusions. Once you ask him about it, he'll tell you and everything will be all right."

"I'm not going to ask him about it. I'm going to wait and see if he tells me. If he doesn't, that's when the real trouble will start."

"You're overreacting. He'll tell you. He would never keep anything from you."

"Maybe. I don't know. I'm going to go upstairs and lie down for a while before meeting Adam and his girlfriend at the club."

"Can I get you anything?"

"Thanks, but no." I got up from the stool, picked up Parker, and went upstairs.

I opened my eyes when I heard the bedroom door open and Alex walked in.

"Hi, sweetheart. Are you okay?" He sat on the edge of the bed and began to rub my back.

"Just a little tired."

Parker went crazy and was jumping at him. He kissed my head, got up and started changing out of his suit.

"How was your day?" I bravely asked.

"Shit. Total shit."

I could tell something was bothering him.

"Why? What happened?" This was his opportunity to tell me.

"Just everything that could go wrong did. Nothing for you to worry about."

Nothing for me to worry about? Was he serious? Was he not going to tell me? Strike one.

"Are you sure you feel well enough to go to the opening of the club?"

"I'm fine. I'm going to take a shower." I climbed out of bed.

"I'll join you." He smiled.

I put my hand up. "No. I started my period today."

"Oh. Okay. I'll just go shower downstairs."

He left the room and I stepped into the shower. I couldn't believe I lied to him about my period. Just as I finished showering, he walked in the bathroom with a towel wrapped around his waist. He was so fucking sexy with his ripped body and soaking wet hair, but the image I saw earlier was playing in my mind over and over like a bad movie.

"Didn't you have your period two weeks ago?" he asked.

"What are you? The period keeper? Fuck, Alex. I can't control when I have my periods."

"Why the attitude, Em? I just asked a simple question and your pills control your period. So obviously, something is wrong."

"Yeah. Maybe something is."

"You need to go see a doctor then."

Oh my God! He wouldn't stop. One little mistruth and he made a huge deal out of it.

"I'll call and make an appointment."

He gave me a small smile and left the bathroom. As I was putting on my makeup, I decided to give him another chance to tell me about today.

"So what happened today? I know you said it was nothing for me to worry about, but I would like to know."

"Just business stuff, Emerson."

Strike two.

He obviously wasn't going to tell me, so I dropped it, for now. I finished getting ready and I could smell his damn cologne infiltrating the bedroom. Shit. Walking into the closet, I slipped into a black and white strapless sundress and had trouble zipping it up.

"Here, let me get that for you," Alex spoke as he walked up behind me and zipped up my dress. His lips softly touched my bare shoulder.

"Thanks."

"Are you ready? Traffic is a bitch at this time and Phillip is waiting for us downstairs."

"Yep. I just need to put on my heels," I spoke as I grabbed them and walked out of the room.

****

Alex

Man, Emerson was certainly PMS'ing tonight. I was worried that she got her period so soon, which also meant no sex for a few days and, after today, I needed her more than ever. I didn't even care if she was on her period, but she did. I didn't attempt to talk to her in the car because it seemed like everything I said was wrong and irritated her. So we rode to the club in silence.

A good friend of mine had opened a karaoke club and we were going to celebrate it. Adam had just met this girl named

Renee a couple of weeks ago and thought it would be the perfect opportunity to introduce her to us. He told us that he really liked her and couldn't wait for us to meet her. Climbing out of the Bentley, I held out my hand to help Emerson out. Surprisingly, she took it and climbed out.

"You look so sexy. Just looking at you is making me hard," I whispered in her ear.

"Sucks to be you," she responded, deadpan.

I sighed. This was going to be a fun night.

Chapter 39

Emerson

He had two chances to tell me and he didn't, so I went into bitch mode. I didn't want to be like that towards him, but I couldn't help it. I was hurt. Deeply hurt. Hurt down to the core of my soul. If he was keeping seeing her a secret, what else was he hiding?

We stepped into the club and I saw Adam by the bar. Thank God. I needed a drink like yesterday.

"There's Adam." Alex pointed.

"I'm not blind," I responded. Alex shot me a look.

The minute we approached the bar, Adam hugged me and shook Alex's hand.

"Renee, this is my sister Emerson and her boyfriend, Alex Parker."

"It's so nice to finally meet you." Renee smiled as we lightly hugged.

Alex leaned over and gave her a kiss on the cheek. "It's nice to meet you."

I bet it was nice to meet her. And that kiss. Really? He couldn't have just shook her hand?

"What do you want to drink?" Alex asked me.

"I'll have a Cosmopolitan."

Renee was a beautiful girl. She stood about five feet four inches with a petite figure, shoulder-length, blonde hair, and green eyes. She had a bubbly personality. She was the type of girl I could easily become best friends with. Too bad I was being such a bitch tonight, compliments of one Alex Parker.

"I'll be right back. I see someone over there I need to talk to," Alex spoke as he kissed my cheek.

Good riddance.

"What the hell is wrong with you tonight? You've been giving Alex stabby eyes since the minute you walked in," Adam said as he lightly grabbed my arm.

"Period."

"Enough said." He rolled his eyes.

I didn't realize I was giving stabby eyes. I'd better cool it. I didn't want to start a scene in front of Alex's friends. It wasn't their fault he was such a douchebag. Finishing off my Cosmopolitan, I ordered another one. Renee and I talked a lot and I really liked her. Even though she and Adam had just met two weeks ago, I could tell they had really fallen for each other.

Alan, the club owner, got up on stage and began to speak.

"I want to thank everyone for coming here tonight to celebrate the opening of my brand new club. Let's get this karaoke started!"

"Are you feeling okay?" Alex asked as he walked up to me.

"Yes. I'm feeling okay, but I'll feel even better after another Cosmo."

"I'll get you one." He smiled.

The four of us sat down as the first person got up and started to sing. Oh my God, he was awful and very drunk. It was quite entertaining.

"Here's your drink, sweetheart."

"Thanks."

"Are you going to get up there?" he asked.

"I think I might." I took a large sip of my drink.

As soon as the drunk guy finished and the alcohol kicked in, I got up from my seat and stepped up on the stage and began to sing "Ex's & Oh's" by Elle King. I found the song extremely appropriate. Everyone started clapping to the beat of the music. When I looked out into the audience, Alex was glaring at me. If looks could kill, I'd be dead. He wasn't happy and I didn't give a damn. Once the song was over, the crowd whistled and clapped. Instead of leaving the stage, I sang the song "Boston" by Augustana. Once I finished, I stumbled back to the table and sat down. Alex lightly grabbed hold of my arm.

"What the fuck were those songs about?" he asked sternly.

"They're just songs. What the hell is your problem?" I glared at him.

"We'll talk about this later." He turned away from me and I noticed Adam and Renee staring at me.

I shrugged and Adam narrowed his eyes at me. I finished off my third Cosmo, started on my fourth, and Alex got up and went to talk to Alan. Getting up from my seat, feeling a bit dizzy, I went up to the bar and asked the sexy bartender to line up two shots of tequila. I threw them back one right after the other and Adam walked up to me.

"What are you doing? I think you've had enough to drink."

"Come on, big brother, where's your fun? Have another shot of tequila with me!" I shouted.

"Seriously, Emerson. You're done."

"What's going on over here?" Alex spoke harshly.

"She's drunk off her ass, Alex. You better get her home. She just downed two shots of tequila."

"Can you walk?" Alex asked me.

"Yes," I slurred.

The look on his face was angry as he lightly took hold of my arm. "Let's go."

"I'm not going anywhere with you as long as you have that attitude." I wiggled out of his grip.

"Emerson, I'm not playing games. Let's go home. Please." He held out his arm.

I hooked my arm in his and tried to make my way through the club. After stumbling a couple of times, Alex picked me up and carried me to the Bentley.

"What were you thinking in there? You normally don't drink like that."

"Can't a girl have a little fun?" I slurred.

"Yes, but not as a sloppy drunk."

"Okay. You win. Everything is spinning and I need you to be quiet."

"Trust me. I will be." He turned and looked out the window.

I laid my head against the window and closed my eyes.

"Phillip, how much longer until we're home?"

"About twenty minutes, Emerson."

Fuck. The movement of the car was making me sick. I heard the gates open and I opened my eyes. Thank God we were home. Alex climbed out, opened my door, and helped me out.

"Come on. Let's get you to bed." He picked me up and carried me as I laid my head on his chest.

"Please don't walk so fast. I'm going to be sick."

"I know. That's why I'm trying to get you upstairs to the bathroom."

When we reached the bedroom, he set me down on the bed. "Are you okay for now or do you need to get to the bathroom?"

I fell over and moaned when my head hit the pillow. I could feel the alcohol make its way up my throat.

"Bathroom! Now!"

I put my hand over my mouth and he hurried me to the bathroom. I gripped the sides of the toilet as he held back my hair.

"I really can't believe you drank so much. We're going to have a long talk about this in the morning."

"You really want to go there, Alex?" I spoke in between vomiting.

"Shh. No more talking."

Once I was finished, Alex helped me up, unzipped my dress and let it fall to the ground. Helping me back to bed, he sat me up and quickly pulled my nightshirt over my head.

"Lie down and sleep it off," he spoke in an irritated tone.

"Don't have to tell me twice." My head hit the pillow.

****

Alex

Perfect end to a shitty day. What the hell was she thinking? I stripped out of my clothes and climbed into bed. I was really pissed off at her and her behavior. And what the fuck were those songs about? I couldn't even begin to comprehend what the hell was going on with her. The one thing I did know was that she better be prepared to explain herself in the morning.

Chapter 40

Emerson

Rolling over, I placed my hand on my forehead and moaned. I heard the door open and Alex sat down on the edge of the bed next to me.

"Are you ready to talk?"

"What time is it?"

"Noon."

Both eyes shot open. "You're kidding, right?"

"No, Emerson. I'm not."

"Shouldn't you be at the office?"

"I've been there and back."

"Ugh. Why didn't you just stay there?" I asked as I looked at him.

"Because we're going to talk about last night."

I closed my eyes so I didn't have to see the anger in his. But then again, he shouldn't want to see the anger in my eyes. Maybe they weren't displaying enough anger and I needed to fix that.

"I smell coffee. Where is it?" I asked with irritation.

"I set it on the dresser. I wasn't sure if you were ready for it." He got up from the bed and grabbed the cup of coffee. "Here."

I glared at him as I sat up with my back against the headboard. "You're not a very good hangover caregiver."

"Excuse me?" He cocked his head with a very small smile.

"Where's the aspirin? You should be bringing me aspirin and water."

He reached into his pocket and shook the bottle of aspirin as he held it in front of me.

"Oh my God, stop making so much noise," I shrieked as I set my coffee on the nightstand, lay back down, and pulled the covers over my head.

He chuckled and pulled the covers back. "Take these aspirin. Here's some water and then we're going to talk."

"Can you at least wait until the aspirin kicks in?" I asked, extremely irritated.

I knew damn well we were headed for our first huge argument and I wanted to not feel like shit when I took him down.

"Fine. I'll give you an hour to get up, shower, and feel better." He kissed my forehead with force.

"That hurt!"

"Good." He winked as he walked out of the room.

After showering and putting on some clothes, I checked Alex's office to see if he was in there. He was. Looking up from his computer, he spoke, "Are you feeling better?"

"Kind of. Are you ready to be taken down, Mr. Parker? Wait, speaking of Parker, where is he?"

"Jenna took him for a walk. And what do you mean am I ready to be taken down?" he asked with a glare in his eye.

"You'll see."

He sighed. "Sit down."

"Nah. I think I'll stand." I folded my arms.

"Emerson, SIT DOWN!" he shouted.

Stand your ground. Don't let him boss you around. This whole argument was stemming because of him. If he only would have told me yesterday about Bella, I wouldn't be standing here right now, hungover and defiant.

"Please, Em. Have a seat and let's talk about this." His voice softened. "Couples need to talk things out."

"But see, Alex, the only thing you want to talk about is last night. About me and how I drank too much. But let me remind you of something. Have you forgotten the night that I had to pick up your drunk ass up at the bar and bring you home? Was that night ever discussed the next day? Or any day for that matter? No. It wasn't. You refused to talk about it, yet that was okay. But now that it's me, it's a different story."

He leaned back in his chair and crossed his arms. "We weren't together and the circumstances then were different."

Okay, he had point, but still, I wasn't backing down.

"What was wrong with you yesterday? And I know damn well it had nothing to do with your period because you're never like that."

I stood there, leaning up against the wall, arms crossed and eyes staring at him. It was time just to lay it all out on the table.

"I went to your office yesterday with lunch to surprise you. When I reached your office, Olivia wasn't at her desk, but your door was slightly open. When I peeked inside, I saw you and Bella locked in a tight embrace. I gave you the opportunity to tell me last night and you didn't. Do you know how that made me feel seeing that? I'm going to tell you something, Parker. You're fucking lucky that I'm still here."

His eyes narrowed at me before he got up from his seat and began to walk over to me.

"Don't you dare come near me," I spoke in anger and he stopped. He knew I was serious.

"I was going to talk to you about that, but I didn't want to last night because we were going to the club."

"Really? You were really going to tell me? It seems to me that you're just saying that because you got caught." I hissed.

"Think what you want, but you're wrong. So that's the reason you drank so much last night?"

"Duh! You would too if you found me in the arms of another man. My God, Alex, I would never put you through that. I just wanted to forget it because that's all I could see. My heart is so broken right now that it even hurts to stand here and look at you." A tear fell from my eye and I wiped it away.

"I'm sorry, baby. Let me hold you."

"No. I don't want you to hold me. I want an explanation. If there even is one. Maybe you've been secretly seeing her behind my back. Maybe everything you've said to me was lies."

"Are you doubting my love for you?" he asked in anger.

"Maybe I am." I looked down.

He placed his hands on his hips and turned his back to me. "We hit one bump in the road and you doubt me and everything we've been through? Do you know how bad that hurts?"

"Not as bad as finding you in the arms of another woman when you supposedly are in love with me."

He whipped himself around and the anger consumed him. "Supposedly? Fuck, Emerson. How can you say that?"

"All I wanted was for you to tell me why she was there."

"And I was going to tell you today. But now, since you believe I don't love you and all of this has meant nothing, there's no need to discuss it because, apparently, you don't believe anything I say. If that's how you feel, then maybe you should leave."

Oh boy, now he really had me fired up. My eyes burned into his. My heart pounded out of my chest and a wave of nausea overtook me as he walked out of the room.

"Hey, Parker!" I yelled.

He turned and looked at me from the hallway. I held both my middle fingers up at him. "Bye, Felicia. By the way, I didn't start my period. I. LIED. TO. YOU!"

He shook his head and walked down the stairs as I went to our bedroom and slammed the door. So much for things being perfect. If it's too good to be true, then it probably is. Isn't that how the quote goes?

I wanted to scream at the top of my lungs. I wanted to throw everything I could get my hands on, but I didn't. I refused to let him break me. I was a fighter and a survivor and, apparently, a very jealous person. You see what he did? He turned it around and blamed me. Did I really doubt his love for me? In a way I did only because he was holding another woman and wouldn't talk about it last night. What else was I supposed to think? I needed to get the fuck out of here for a while. I needed to clear my head and really think about what had just happened and I couldn't do that in this house. I was heading down the only road I'd ever known.

Chapter 41

Alex

I went out the back door and down to the beach. I needed just to cool down. For her not to believe that I loved her killed me like nothing ever had. If she never would have seen me and Bella, we wouldn't be having this argument. I would have told her today why she was there and she would have understood. She was hurt by what she saw, but to doubt that I loved her was crossing the line with me. I had given her everything I had. My heart, my soul, my world, and in one lousy fucking moment, she doubted me. That right there hurt me to the very core of my existence.

About a mile up the beach was a waterfront restaurant. I needed a drink to calm down and to think, so I walked there. Sitting at the bar for a couple of hours, sipping on the same drink, something hit me. I told her to leave. Panic settled inside me because that was exactly what she'd do. I never should have walked away from her and I shouldn't have been so stubborn and not tell her the truth. I threw some money on the bar and ran up the beach back to my house. I ran as fast as I could as the wind swept across my face and the ocean roared. I flew in the back door and up the stairs to our bedroom. The door was open and Emerson wasn't in there. I looked in the closet to see her suitcase gone and empty hangers hanging where her clothes hung. Slamming my hand against the molding of the door, I yelled, "Emerson!"

Jenna came running into the bedroom and looked at me. She knew something. I could see it in her sad eyes.

"Where is she?" I asked through gritted teeth.

"I don't know, Alex. She just said that she needed to think and clear her head."

"She can't fucking do that here in California?"

"Calm down. You don't know if she left the state. Maybe she went to Adam's house."

"Maybe she did. I'll give him a call."

I pulled out my phone and dialed Adam.

"Hey, Alex, what's up?"

"Adam, have you talked to Emerson by chance?"

"No. I was going to call her later to find out how she was feeling. Why?"

"Are you home?"

"Yeah. What's going on, man?"

"We got into a huge fight and her suitcase is gone and so are some of her clothes."

"Shit, Alex. What the hell happened?"

"It's a long story and I'd rather not get into it right now. Could you do me a favor and give her a call? If I call her, she won't answer."

"Sure thing. I'll call you back." *Click.*

Suddenly, I heard her phone go off. I looked at Jenna and she looked at me. It sounded like it was coming from the nightstand. I walked over, opened the drawer, and saw her phone sitting there. I answered the call from Adam.

"It's me. She left her phone here."

"Ah, fuck! Find her, Alex. Do whatever you have to and find her. I don't trust that she'll come back, especially if she's hurting."

"I will. I'll keep you posted."

Looking over at Jenna, who was shooting me a nasty look, I walked over to the closet and took the map down she had stored up on the shelf. Laying it on the bed, I spoke, "Let's see if we can figure out where she went off to."

As we looked over the map, nothing was looking right. I sighed as I sat down on the bed. Suddenly, the song she sang at karaoke last night crept into my mind.

"Jenna, Emerson sang a song last night at the club and she was staring at me the whole time she sang it. Something about Boston."

"Hmm. Let me google it. Hold on."

She pulled her phone out and looked at me. "Is this the song she was singing?" she asked as she played the song.

"YES! That's it. I will bet my life on it that's where she went. She's heading to Boston. Pull up the flight schedule and see what the next flight is. There's no way she got on a plane already."

"It says here that the next flight leaves in thirty minutes," she spoke.

"That's the one she has to be on. Is it nonstop?"

"Yes and it's a five-hour flight."

"Okay. If I leave now, I can catch her at the airport in Boston." I ran to the closet, pulled out my carryon bag, and packed a few things. Pulling out my phone, I called my pilot.

"Get the plane ready NOW! We're going to Boston."

"It'll be ready and waiting, sir."

****

Emerson

What am I doing? I thought to myself as I sat on the sand in Venice Beach. I watched as couples walked along the shoreline hand in hand, laughing and kissing. Looking around, I took notice of the families all around. Parents were having fun with their kids, chasing them around, and helping them build sand castles. I knew Alex would make a wonderful father someday, even though we never once talked about children. Hell, I didn't know if he even wanted any kids. But I did. I wanted a family like I grew up with. It was something that Emily and I always talked about before the accident. We'd talk about how we would get married and our children would grow up together. That dream died the day of the accident, but resurfaced when I fell in love with Alex.

God, I was stupid for acting the way I did. I didn't doubt that he loved me. I really didn't. I was hurt so deeply and, in some way, I wanted him to feel my pain. Two wrongs didn't make a right and I was a fool for saying what I did. I had planned to spend a couple of days here in Venice Beach just to clear my thoughts and my head. But I changed my mind and I hadn't made a room reservation yet because I stopped at the beach first. Digging through my purse, I noticed my phone wasn't in there. When I reached the car, I looked to see if maybe it had fallen on the floor. I looked under the seats and it wasn't there. Shit. I didn't remember taking it out of the nightstand drawer because I was in such a hurry to get out of there. I hopped in the car and drove back home to apologize to Alex and beg for his forgiveness. Okay, I wasn't going to beg, but I was sure going to make him see how sorry I was.

****

Alex

Sitting on the plane, my phone was almost dead, so I turned it off, pulled out my charger, and plugged it in. There was no need to have it on since Emerson didn't have hers with her. She probably left it on purpose so I couldn't contact her, which made me angry. But I didn't blame her. I was nothing but a douchebag. No, actually, I was a fucker, and I was going to make things right the minute I found her in Boston. I made a promise to her that she would never travel alone again and I broke that promise when I told her to leave. I just prayed to God that my plane got in before hers so I could catch her at the airport. She had to be on that flight. It was the next available one and the time frame worked out. She would have had plenty of time to get to the airport and board before it took off. I rested my hand on my forehead and closed my eyes.

Chapter 42

Emerson

Walking into the house, Parker greeted me. As I bent down to pet him, Jenna walked into the foyer with a surprised look on her face.

"Emerson. What are you doing here? You're supposed to be on your way to Boston."

"Huh?" I asked in confusion. "Why would I be going to Boston? I was in Venice Beach and decided that I needed to come home."

"Oh fuck!" she said.

"What? Where's Alex?"

She gulped. "On his way to Boston to find you."

I shook my head because I didn't understand what the hell was going on. "What do you mean he's on his way to Boston? Where did he get the idea that I went to Boston?"

"From a song you sang last night." She bit down on her bottom lip.

Suddenly, my eyes widened. "Oh shit!" I ran up the stairs and pulled my phone from the nightstand, quickly dialing him.

It went straight to voicemail. "Shit. It went straight to voicemail."

"He probably doesn't have service up in the air."

"Oh my God, could this day get any worse? I need to go to Boston." I pulled up the flight schedule and the next flight out was in three hours, but it was sold out. The next flight was with a connecting flight in Minneapolis, which put it at almost eight hours and that flight didn't leave for another four hours. The next nonstop flight didn't leave until tomorrow morning.

"Why don't you just wait until tomorrow morning to fly out?"

"No. I can't wait. I have to get on a plane now."

"But you won't get in until four a.m. That's dangerous. You can't be walking the streets of Boston in the middle of the night."

I sighed. "What about his private jet?"

"He's on it now. You're really going to make his pilot fly another five hours back to Boston?"

"Damn it! I suppose you're right. Well, I'll just get in at four a.m. and get a room at the airport until I figure out where he is. I can't stay here all night. I'll go crazy." I booked the flight that was leaving in four hours.

****

Alex

The plane landed at the airport and I raced off it, running to a monitor to see which gate her flight was at. Of course her flight had just landed and her gate was at the other end of the terminal. I ran through the airport like a madman.

"Excuse me. The flight that just landed, have all the passengers gotten off already?"

"Yes, sir. We just shut the doors. Everyone is off the plane."

"Thank you." I sighed as I looked around and then headed to baggage claim. She wasn't there. But then again, her carryon bag was gone from the closet, so she probably didn't check a bag. As I sat down on one of the benches, I went to pull my phone from my pocket and noticed it wasn't there. FUCK! I forgot to grab it before I got off the plane. Could this day get any worse? I cupped my face in my hands.

I hailed a cab and had the driver take me to my hotel, Parker International. As I walked through the lobby doors, the employees stared at me with frightened looks on their faces. I gave a small wave and took the elevator up to my penthouse suite. Setting my bag down, I poured myself a drink and headed back down to the lobby.

"It's nice to see you again, Mr. Parker." Todd smiled at me from behind the desk. "We didn't know you were planning a visit."

"It was very last minute. Listen, Todd, I need you to do me a favor."

"Anything, sir."

"I need you to tap into the system of all the hotels in the Boston area and find out if a woman named Emerson James checked in anywhere."

"I'm sorry, sir, but the only person who can do that is Wes, and he's gone for the night."

"Well then, call Wes at home and tell him I need him here. It's an emergency."

"Yes, sir. Right away."

I looked at my watch. It was nine o'clock. "Also, have a filet, medium rare, with a baked potato and green beans sent up to the penthouse."

"Right away, sir."

****

Emerson

My flight from Minneapolis was delayed an hour and finally ready to take off. I laid my head against the window as I thought about Alex. I couldn't believe he thought I was going to Boston. Those damn cocktails I had last night. I wondered what he was doing, where he was, and how pissed off he was because he couldn't find me. Even if I was in Boston, how the hell would he find me? Would he scour every hotel in the area looking for me? God, I loved that man so much and to put him through this tore me apart. Then again, he was the one who just assumed I went to Boston, so technically, it wasn't my fault. He shouldn't have gone assuming things. But with my pattern, I didn't blame him. Boy, did I have some serious making up to do for this one. I closed my eyes to get some sleep.

****

Alex

As I was eating dinner, there was a knock at the door. When I opened it, Wes was standing there.

"Good evening, sir."

"Good evening, Wes. Thank you for coming here."

"The front desk said it was an emergency."

"Yes. I need you to tap into all the hotel systems in the Boston area and find out if Emerson James has checked into any of the hotels."

"I can do that. May I use the laptop on the desk?"

"Certainly."

He took a seat at the desk and began typing on the laptop.

"May I get you a drink?" I asked.

"I'm fine, sir. Thank you. It doesn't look like she has checked in anywhere."

"Impossible. She had to have."

"I'm sorry, sir, but her name isn't anywhere in the databases."

"Great. I wonder if she checked in under a different name knowing that I would be looking for her. Try Emily James."

He slowly shook his head. "I'm sorry, but she's not checked in either."

"Thank you for your help, Wes. I'll make sure to compensate you well for this unexpected visit."

"No need, sir. I'm just doing my job."

I gave him a small smile as I led him to the door. Reaching into my pocket, I pulled out two one-hundred-dollar bills and placed it in his hand.

"Take this and thank you."

"Thank you, sir. Have a good night."

I shut the door and went into the bedroom. Opening my bag, I removed the small blue box from it and opened it. Where are you, Emerson?

Chapter 43

Emerson

I finally landed at five a.m. Good God, I needed coffee. Once I got off the plane, I found a Starbucks and ordered a coffee with a double shot of espresso. Taking it to one of the tables, I sat down and pulled out my phone. Now what? It wasn't like I could do much at this hour. I drank my coffee and then headed to the bathroom to freshen up. I was a hot mess with mascara stains underneath my eyes. After removing my makeup, I reapplied it and then brushed my hair. If I was going to find Alex, I wanted to make sure I looked good for him. I kept trying to call him all night and it still went to voicemail and I was starting to get worried. It wasn't like him to have his phone off. Now that it was seven a.m., it was time to start looking for him, but where did I start? If he got in yesterday, then he would have gotten a room somewhere. I called Adam.

"Where the hell are you? I've been worried sick."

"I'm fine. You all have totally blown everything out of proportion and I'll explain it to you when I see you. But first, I need to know if Alex has a hotel here in Boston?"

"I think he does. Hold on, let me make sure. Yes. It's called Parker International and it's across from the Ritz Carlton on

Avery Street. It's about a fifteen-minute drive, but you're going to be in rush hour, so it may take a little longer."

"Thanks, Adam. I love you."

"I love you too and we're going to talk when you get back."

I sighed. "I know."

Walking out of the airport, I hailed a cab and had the driver take me to Parker International. As I stepped into the lobby, I went up to the desk.

"Hello, welcome to Parker International. How may I help you?"

"I'm looking for Mr. Alex Parker. Is he here?"

"I'm sorry, but I can't give you that information."

A nice-looking man walked over and smiled at me. "You wouldn't happen to be Miss Emerson James, would you?"

A smile crossed my lips. "Yes, I am."

"I'll just need to see some identification, if you don't mind."

I reached into my purse and pulled out my driver's license and handed it to the man named Wes.

He glanced at my I.D. and, with a smile, he handed it back to me. "Here's the elevator key to get to the penthouse. It's on the top floor. Mr. Parker has been looking for you."

"I know. Thank you." I smiled.

I headed to the elevators, inserted the card, and took it up to the top floor. When the doors opened, I stepped into the hallway and stood before the large, double wooden doors. Taking in a deep breath, I lightly knocked. The door opened and Alex stood there with a shocked look on his face.

"I heard you were looking for me." I grinned nervously.

He grabbed me and pulled me inside. Our mouths smashed into each other as our tongues danced with happiness. His hands were firmly planted on each side of my face as our kiss was never ending.

"Thank God, you're safe." He smiled as he kept kissing my lips.

"Of course I'm safe. I'm a seasoned traveler."

He chuckled and held me tight. "Where have you been? I've been trying to search the city for you. You didn't check into any hotels."

"I didn't get into Boston until a couple of hours ago."

"What?" he asked as he broke our embrace.

"You idiot!" I lightly smacked his chest. "I wasn't coming to Boston. I went to Venice Beach. I was only going to stay there for a couple of days to think and then I missed your dumb ass too much and after a couple of hours I went home."

"Oh. But you left without your phone."

"Yeah. I forgot it in my mad dash to leave the house. And speaking of phones, I've been trying since yesterday to call you."

"I turned it off to let it charge and I left it on the plane because I was trying to get to your gate to catch you before you left the airport."

"Sorry, but I wasn't there. I was back in California!"

"The only thing that matters is you're here and you're safe." He pulled me back into a tight embrace.

"Alex, I'm so sorry for everything I said. I didn't mean any of it."

He placed his hand on my cheek. "Don't. I'm the one who's sorry. I should have told you that night. My God, Em, I love you so much and I never want you to doubt that."

"I know, and I love you too, and I don't doubt it. I never did. I was just being a bitch."

"You're not a bitch, sweetheart. You're the love of my life and the only woman I want to spend the rest of my life with." He smiled. "Are you hungry? I was just about to order breakfast."

"I am, but we can eat after we have the best make-up sex on the planet." I smiled.

"That's exactly what I was thinking." He picked me up and carried me to the bedroom.

****

Alex

She blew my mind. I didn't think sex with her could get any better than it already was and I was dead wrong. We lay there, trying to catch our breath and smiling at each other. As we both climbed out of bed, we slipped on our robes and I ordered us breakfast.

"We need to talk, baby. I need to tell you about why Bella was at my office that day," I spoke as I took her hand and led her to the couch.

"I know and I'm ready to talk about it."

A smile crossed my lips as I kissed her. "Shortly after she left for New York, she found out she was pregnant and I was the father. Instead of telling me, she went and had an abortion."

"Oh my God, Alex." She placed her hand on my cheek. "I don't know what to say except I'm sorry."

"She told me she had been ridden with guilt for the past five years and she said that she needed to tell me with the hopes that I would forgive her because she couldn't forgive herself."

"Did you forgive her?"

"Yes. I was angry at first that she would do something like that without talking to me. But after we talked a bit and I could see how upset she was, I forgave her. I suppose she suffered in silence enough over the past five years. That's when you must have seen us hugging. It meant nothing, Emerson. It was a friendly hug goodbye."

"I feel so stupid, Alex. I'm so sorry."

"Don't apologize. I understand why you felt the way you did because if I saw you hugging one of your exes, I would have jumped to the same conclusions. I should have come right home and told you, but I didn't want to upset you or ruin our evening at the club. I swear I was going to tell you that next morning."

"You don't need to explain anything else to me." She leaned over and kissed my lips.

There was a knock at the door and room service had arrived. I got up and answered it and we sat and talked some more while we ate breakfast. After making love in bed and in the shower, we got dressed and headed out to explore Boston. But before heading out, I left her standing in the lobby while I had to quickly do something.

Chapter 44

Emerson

Alex and I spent a wonderful day together in Boston. We visited a couple museums, Fenway Park, the aquarium, and we did some shopping. He was spoiling me and I wasn't complaining.

"We should get back to the hotel and change for dinner," he spoke.

"Good idea. I'm getting hungry."

He hooked his arm around me and kissed the side of my head. "I love you, Emerson James."

"I love you too, Alex Parker."

When we arrived back at the hotel, Alex opened the door and I stepped in first. I gasped as I looked around the room. Rose petals were scattered all over the floor and across the dining table where two beautifully lit candles flickered.

"What's all this?" I smiled as I looked at him.

"I thought we could have a romantic dinner in the room tonight."

"This is beautiful. Thank you." I kissed him.

"You're welcome. Now let's sit down and eat."

He took hold of my hand, led me to the table, and pulled out my chair.

"When did you arrange all this?" I asked.

"This morning before we left."

"You're such a romantic."

"Only for you." He winked.

I lifted the elegantly designed silver top off the tray and lying there, on a small crystal plate, was the most beautiful ring I'd ever seen in my life. I threw my hands over my mouth as I looked at Alex with tears in my eyes.

Smiling at me, he got up from his seat, took the ring from the plate, and got down on one knee, taking hold of my left hand.

"Emerson, I have never loved anyone in my lifetime until you came along and took my breath away. You have given me so much and you've taught me things I would have never known if I hadn't met you. You've given my life meaning and purpose. I can't ever imagine my life without you in it and I never want to. You complete me as a man and I will love you to the moon and back for the rest of my life. You're my queen and I want to be your king. Will you marry me, Emerson?"

I was shaking and I couldn't control the tears that were falling in front of this beautiful man. A man who had changed me and my way of life. A man who had given himself completely to me and I to him. Life without Alex wouldn't be possible.

"Yes. Of course I'll marry you!"

He let out a breath and placed the ring on my finger. "I love you more than life, Emerson."

"I love you more than life, Alex." I smiled as we both stood up and hugged each other tightly.

****

The next morning, we headed back to California. I couldn't wait to tell Adam the good news. As we were sitting on the couch on the plane, sipping champagne, I held out my hand and looked at my stunning two-carat princess cut, diamond-encased ring.

"Do you like it?" Alex asked.

"I love it. You have amazing taste."

"The moment I saw it, I knew it would look gorgeous on you."

"I'm surprised you didn't take it back after my bitch act that day."

He chuckled. "I would never have taken it back. I love you too much, smart mouth, bitchiness and all." He kissed my lips.

"So how about we set a date right now?" I spoke.

"Really?" He smiled. "If I could have married you in Boston, I would have."

"Let's go to Vegas and get married instead of going back to Cali."

"Nah. You stripped there."

"True." I smirked.

"What kind of wedding do you want?" he asked as he stroked my cheek with his finger.

"I don't care. As long as we say 'I do,' it doesn't matter."

"Haven't you always dreamed of a beautiful wedding?"

"Yeah. I have."

"Then a beautiful wedding is what you're getting. No expense will be spared. How about we get married on the beach."

"Which beach?" I asked.

"Any beach you want. We can stay in California, fly off to Hawaii or some other island. It's up to you."

"I would like to get married in California." I smiled.

"I was hoping you'd say that. We'll pick a place together. Although I don't want to wait too long. I want you as Mrs. Alex Parker as soon as possible."

"Who said I was taking your last name?"

He cocked his head in surprise. "You *are* taking my last name."

"Says who?"

"Says me. Your fiancé."

I leaned over and brushed my lips against his. "I just wanted to hear you say it."

"Emerson, I swear, one day, you will be the death of me."

I laughed. "At least you'll die happy."

"Very happy." He smiled as we passionately kissed.

Chapter 45

Emerson

Six Months Later

Our wedding day. Alex and I decided to get married at Meadowood in Napa Valley. As much as we loved the beach, we picked a place that had a special meaning to us and Napa was one of those places. Besides, we both loved wine and what better place to get married than surrounded by vineyards and wineries.

I stood in front of the full-length mirror and stared at my elegant white strapless, sweetheart neckline, delicate lace and beaded mermaid-style dress. I couldn't believe this day had finally come and I was about to become Mrs. Alex Parker.

"You look so beautiful." Jenna smiled with a tear in her eye.

"Thank you. I'm so nervous."

"Don't be. Just think of how nervous Alex is right now."

"True. He's probably more nervous than I am." I lightly laughed.

"Wow. Wow. Wow. Look at you!" Adam exclaimed as he stepped inside the room. Tears began to fill his eyes.

"God, Adam, don't get all weepy."

"I have something for you."

"What is it?" I smiled.

He reached in his pocket and pulled out a silver bracelet with a small diamond heart dangling from it.

"This was Mom's. Do you remember it?"

"Yes. She only wore it on special occasions."

"I remember sitting in her room one night while she was getting ready to go out with Dad. It was their anniversary. She had asked me to help her put it on and she told me that she was going to pass it on to you and Emily on your wedding days. After they died, I found it when I was cleaning out her jewelry box and I saved it because I knew someday you'd want to wear it."

A tear fell from my eye as he put it on my wrist. "It's something old and now it's yours." He wiped the tear from my eye. "I couldn't be more proud to take Dad's place and walk you down the aisle." More tears started to fill my eyes. "Don't cry. Please. If I hand you over to Alex with mascara under your eyes, he'll kill me."

I laughed and looked up at the ceiling to prevent the tears from falling. "Thank you, Adam."

"You're welcome, Emerson." He held out his arm. "It's time. Are you ready?"

I took in a deep breath. "Yes. I am more than ready."

The set-up outside was stunning. White chairs for 250 people were lined up on each side of the grass. At the end of the walkway stood two stands that housed beautiful tall floral arrangements in white flowers. Beyond the small stone wall that sat in front of us was the most beautiful view of the vineyards. The music began to play as Renee walked down the aisle and took her place as my bridesmaid. Jenna followed as my maid of honor next to Parker, who carried the rings around his neck. The bridal march began and I held my breath for a moment.

"Let's get you to your future husband." Adam smiled as he gave my hand around his arm a gentle squeeze.

I couldn't focus on anything but Alex as I walked with Adam down the aisle. The grin on his face told me everything. When we reached the end of the aisle, Adam took my hand and placed it in Alex's and then he took his place by his side.

"You're so beautiful," he whispered.

"So are you."

The minister spoke a few words and then Alex and I said our vows. After saying "I do" and placing the ring on each other's fingers, we were pronounced husband and wife.

"You may kiss your beautiful bride, Alex."

He smiled as he leaned over and our lips locked tightly, sharing our very first kiss as husband and wife. Our guests clapped and whistled as the music played and we walked up the aisle hand in hand. This was the most magical day of my life.

****

Alex

Seeing my wife in that dress was the most beautiful sight I'd ever seen. She was glowing from head to toe and she made me the happiest man alive. After our vows, our guests went inside the big white fabric tent that was lined with lights, elegantly decorated tables and fresh flowers. Emerson and I headed over by the lake where swans swam to take pictures.

"How does it feel to be Mrs. Alex Parker?" I asked.

"It feels amazing. Keep calling me that. It turns me on." She winked.

The best part of the night was yet to come when I could take her back to the suite and make love to her for the first time as my wife. Once pictures were over, we joined our guests inside the tent, where we celebrated the night away with an elegant dinner, fine wine and cocktails, and dancing.

We didn't have the typical first dance song that most wedding couples did. Our song was "Don't Look back in Anger" by Oasis. When the song began to play, the video of Emily and Emerson singing began to play on the big screen I had the staff set up. I held out my hand and Emerson joined me on the dance floor where we both sang the song together and danced our first dance as husband and wife. As soon as our dance ended, it started to lightly rain. Emerson looked at me with a wide grin splayed across her face and the band began to play a slow song. I grabbed her hand and led her outside the tent. Placing my hand around her waist, and with her hand on my shoulder, we danced together in the rain.

Chapter 46

Emerson

Eight Months Later

My eyes flew open and I grabbed Alex's arm.

"What's wrong?" he asked.

"My water just broke."

"Are you sure you just didn't pee the bed, sweetheart?"

"Are you serious right now? I would know if I peed the bed."

"But you thought that a couple of weeks ago and you peed the bed."

"Get up and examine it then." I lightly smacked his arm.

He sat up and turned on the light. Pulling the covers back, his eyes widened.

"Oh shit, that's not pee."

"I told you!"

I tried to get up from the bed and couldn't. I was huge and trying to move around these days was nearly impossible. Alex took hold of my hands and helped me up. He grabbed a pair of new underwear from the drawer and held them up.

"Not to be rude, baby, but I can't wait until you get rid of these."

"I know, right?" I agreed with him.

He grabbed my dress from the closet and helped me get into it.

"Are you in any pain?"

"No. Not yet."

"That's good. Then the car ride should be smooth."

I rolled my eyes as he grabbed my suitcase and we climbed into the car. We were about a half hour away from the hospital when the first contraction hit.

"Holy fuck me now! OH MY GOD!" I screamed as I grabbed Alex's arm and dug my nails into him.

"Breathe, Em. In and out. In and out," he spoke as he placed his hand on my belly.

I did as he said and it wasn't working. Finally, the contraction subsided. We reached the hospital and I was wheeled up to the Labor and Delivery unit.

"Do you want me to call Adam?"

"Yes. He'll kill us both if we don't. He said he and Renee would be here."

Once I got into the room, a nurse named Kelly introduced herself to me and Alex. She helped me into one of those god awful hospital gowns and hooked me up to the fetal monitor. Another contraction hit and I let out a loud howl.

"Breathe, Em. In and out. In and out. In and out." He hovered over me.

"I swear to God, Parker, if you say in and out one more time, I'm going to break your balls so you can never do this to me again!"

Kelly, the nurse, laughed. "It's okay, Mr. Parker. I've heard it all. I'm going to call your doctor, Emerson. I think he's already here at the hospital delivering another baby."

The contraction subsided and I could finally breathe.

"Adam and Renee are on their way. I'm afraid to ask how you are."

"I'm sorry, Alex. OH MY GOD, I HATE YOU RIGHT NOW!" I screamed as another contraction hit and I squeezed the living hell out of his hand.

Dr. Williams walked in and looked at me. "Breathe through it, Emerson. In and out."

"Oh, he can say that to you, but I can't," Alex spoke.

"We aren't discussing this now," I spoke through gritted teeth.

Dr. Williams examined me and then told me that if I wanted an epidural, now was the time to have it.

"We agreed that she wasn't going to have an epidural," Alex spoke.

Another contraction was starting and I couldn't hold back. "I want the epidural," I panted.

"But, baby, we talked about this and you said no drugs. It wasn't good for the baby."

"I WANT THE DRUGS!" I yelled. "Are you the one lying here while your insides are being ripped to pieces?"

Alex took a step back. "She'll take the epidural," he spoke.

A few moments later, the anesthesiologist walked in and gave me the epidural. It was painful but nothing compared to the contractions I was having. Relief finally settled throughout me and I felt as if I could relax.

"Alex." I softly stroked his arm. "I'm sorry." I pouted.

He leaned over and kissed my forehead. "It's okay, baby. Soon we'll be holding our daughter in our arms."

I smiled at him as Dr. Williams walked back in to examine me again.

"It's time, Emerson. You are fully dilated and it's time to start pushing. Are you ready?"

"Yes. I am more than ready to get this child out of me."

"She didn't really mean that," Alex spoke to the doctor.

"Yes I did. Why are you saying that I didn't really mean it? Did you carry this child for the last nine months? Did you feel the uncontrollable need to pee every second of the day? Did your feet swell up like balloons? Did you have constant heartburn? Were you exhausted before you even woke up in the mornings?"

"Baby, you need to be quiet now and start pushing," he said as he grabbed my hand.

"Don't tell me to be quiet."

"On the count of three, Emerson," Dr. Williams said. "One, two, three, push."

I strained and pushed as hard as I could. After the third push, I was so exhausted that I couldn't do it anymore. I lay back and tried to catch my breath.

"Emerson, you have to push again," Dr. Williams spoke.

"I can't. I just can't do it anymore. I'm so tired."

Alex leaned over and kissed me. "Yes you can. You can do this, Em, and I'm going to help you. Now sit up and push. Do it for me, baby. I can't wait to meet our daughter."

I sat up as he held my hand and gave it everything I had.

"That's it. I see her head. One more big push and she'll be out," Dr. Williams spoke.

"Come on, Emerson. One more time. Just one more time for us. For our daughter."

I screamed as I pushed as hard as I could, my insides tearing apart and, suddenly, she was out and I heard her first cry.

"You did it, baby. You did it. Look at her. She's beautiful." Alex smiled as tears streamed down his face.

I fell back with relief as Dr. Williams laid my baby girl on me. I reached up and touched her hand as she cried her little lungs out. Alex cut the cord and Kelly took her to clean her up and weigh her. After wrapping her tightly in a blanket, she laid her in my arms.

"Hi, Lia Emily Parker." I smiled as I kissed her tiny head.

"She has your beautiful lips." Alex smiled as he kissed her. "I can't wait to introduce her to the penguins."

I looked over at him in confusion. "What?"

"You know, the penguins. From *Madagascar*?"

****

It had been a couple of weeks since we brought Lia home from the hospital. I was recovering quickly and Alex was the best daddy in the world. Seeing him with her always left me breathless. As much as I wanted to breast feed, it just wasn't working out, so her pediatrician put her on formula. Alex would get up most nights and feed her because he couldn't stand to be away from her for too long. Every whimper she made, he'd run to her side. He took a three-month leave from the office and worked from home, only attending meetings when necessary. As for Parker, he was getting used to the cries that now infiltrated his once quiet home.

We were already planning our next trip as a family. It was no longer just me traveling around the world and it was no longer just the two of us. Now, it was the three of us traveling together and we couldn't wait to show our daughter the beauty the world had to offer. I never thought when I stepped through the doors of this house for the very first time that Alex Parker would be the man who would change my life forever.

****

Alex

Three Months Later

Emerson had some errands to run and left Lia home with me. It was just the two of us and I had big plans for our day. After preparing a bottle for her, I carried her into the living room and turned on *Madagascar*.

"You're going to love this movie, Lia." I smiled at her as I held her up and kissed her cheek. She cooed and my heart melted just like it did every time she made a sound.

After feeding her, I sat her up and held her against me while we watched the movie. As soon as the penguins came on, she laughed. I swear to God, she laughed for the very first time. Oh shit. Emerson was going to kill me if I told her. While we were sitting there enjoying the movie, Emerson walked in.

"What's going on here?" She smiled as she sat down next to us.

"I have introduced our daughter to King Julian." I smirked.

"Liar! You introduced her to the penguins," she laughed.

"So what if I did? She happens to like the penguins."

She leaned over, kissed Lia on the head and then brought her lips up to mine.

"I love you," she whispered.

"And I love you, baby."

The penguins appeared on the screen and Lia let out a laugh. Emerson's eyes widened.

"Did she just laugh?"

I had to fake a surprise reaction. "I think so. Our little girl just laughed for the first time, Em."

She took her from my arms and held her up. “Did you just laugh at the penguins?”

Lia cooed and then began to cry. Emerson looked at me and frowned.

“See, Em. She wants to see the penguins. You better turn her around before she goes into a fit of rage.” I smiled.

Emerson rolled her eyes as she held Lia facing the TV. I put my arm around her and pulled them close to me.

“Are you sure you don’t want to come over to the penguin side?” I asked.

“Never. It’s King Julian forever!” She grinned.

Being a husband and a father to the most incredible girls in the world was every man’s dream and I was living it. Life was perfect and my family was perfect. The day Emerson James walked through the front doors of my home, my life changed forever. A change that made me the man I was today.

About the Author

Sandi Lynn is a New York Times, USA Today, and Wall Street Journal bestselling author who spends all of her days writing. She published her first novel, Forever Black, in February 2013 and hasn't stopped writing since. Her addictions are shopping, going to the gym, romance novels, coffee, chocolate, margaritas, and giving readers an escape to another world.

Please come connect with her at:

www.facebook.com/Sandi.Lynn.Author

www.twitter.com/SandilynnWriter

www.authorsandilynn.com

www.pinterest.com/sandilynnWriter

www.instagram.com/sandilynnauthor

https://www.goodreads.com/author/show/6089757.Sandi_Lynn

19745955R20166

Printed in Great Britain
by Amazon